Crazed Reckoning

Valerie J. Clarizio

Published by
Melange Books, LLC
White Bear Lake, MN 55110
www.melange-books.com

To Aunt Germaine and Uncle Myron, and Uncle Dan and Aunt Marge,
thanks for everything.
Love always, Val

Chapter One

Shannon studied her handheld global positioning unit before tossing a glance over her shoulder at Anna. "According to the coordinates, we're exactly where we are supposed to be."

"Great, now, we just need to find our little treasure," Anna replied with an excited schoolgirl grin usually reserved for Christmas morning.

The ladies scavenged the area looking for the cache. What would it look like? How big would it be? And most importantly, would they be able to decipher the clue inside, leading them to the ultimate treasure. She imagined her and Anna wearing the two 14 karat gold Claddagh friendship rings, the grand prize for their club's "Saint Patrick's Day Women's Geocaching Weekend Adventure" in beautiful Door County, Wisconsin.

Shannon's pulse raced and her eyes rapidly shifted back and forth, as she scanned her surroundings. "We need to hurry," she informed Anna as if her friend already didn't know they were competing against nine other teams of two.

According to the instructions, four caches contained numeric clues. Once located and deciphered, they provided the coordinates leading to the fifth cache, the prize cache.

"I'm looking as fast as I can," Anna replied with a tinge of annoyance in her voice. Yet she kept her smile in place. "Is someone just a bit excited?"

Shannon giggled. "I'm sorry. I guess I am."

Frigid air nipped at Shannon's nose as she stood at the edge of the four-foot high rock cliff lining the icy waters of the bay. Ice chunks of all shapes and sizes rushed past the ledge and rode the waves into the unforgiving ledge. Some broke into pieces as they struck the hard rock and sent a thunderous reverberation into the atmosphere with such force that Shannon's chest vibrated in response.

Shannon yanked her zipper up until it reached her chin, and then she pulled her headband over her already frozen ears. She glanced at Anna who had already done the same. "I'm sure glad I wore my Columbia jacket and ski pants on this adventure. I nearly didn't, but then I remembered how Mother Nature tended to let loose her frustration in Door County in March."

Anna nodded. "Last year it was nearly sixty degrees on this weekend. This morning the weatherman predicted a high of thirty-five. What a difference."

Shannon pulled her phone from her pocket to snap a couple pictures. "It's so beautiful here."

"All the state parks in Door County are gorgeous, but I have to admit, this one is my favorite. My parents used to take my siblings and me camping here. And it wasn't the kind of camping people do nowadays with campers, Dish TV and handheld video games. It was the 'pitch the tent' kind with hiking and fishing." Anna stepped closer to the edge and pointed to the left. "There's a boat ramp over there. My dad would launch his little rowboat and we'd catch perch and sunfish. It was fun."

Shannon fixed her gaze on Anna as she stared out over the water. She looked content, lost in fond childhood memories.

A twig snapped. A rustling sound followed from the same direction the women had just come. Shannon spun around. "Did you hear that?"

Anna peered into the woods as well.

Though just past noon, the overcast day darkened the woods as if it were early evening.

The wind whipped around them. Trees swayed and creaked.

"It was probably just the wind," Anna assured.

"Yeah," Shannon whispered, though a hint of unease coiled around her spine.

Anna shifted her gaze. "Well, it's got to be here somewhere," she commented before she dropped to all fours and leaned over the ledge. Her neck craned to see if anything was stashed beneath the overhang.

Anna looked up, grinning like a kid in a candy store. "It's hanging under there but I don't think I can reach it."

Shannon knelt in the soft melting snow and leaned over the edge to take a look. She stretched out her arm, gripped the red cylinder, and handed it to Anna. Anna twisted off the top and pulled the small notepad from the container. After she signed the log, she ripped out the page addressed to their team and refastened the top to the container. Shannon returned the cylinder to where she'd found it.

"Hmm," they sounded in unison as they glanced at the clue. It meant nothing to them at the moment. They'd feed it into the deciphering software Shannon had purchased once they gathered all the clues from the four caches.

As they walked back toward their car, they discovered a marked trail. "Excellent, a trail," Anna commented. "It sure would have been handy if the GPS had taken us in on it rather than the roundabout way we took."

Shannon brought up the park map on her phone. "Looks like this trail will take us right back to the parking lot, but if we stay on the trail our fresh footprints will be a dead giveaway to the teams that follow us." Shannon thought for a moment and then shrugged. "On the flipside, perhaps our next search will be made easier by *our* predecessors' trail." Hmm, easy or adventure? She forged on; she wanted the grand prize.

Anna sucked in a loud breath. Shannon glanced over her shoulder. She didn't know if her friend's cheeks were rosy from the exertion or the wind. "I caught a glimpse of a bench up ahead. Do you want to take five?"

Anna nodded. "Yeah, I'm not as young as I used to be."

Their hike to the cache hadn't been a long one, but the terrain they crossed didn't make for an easy walk. They stepped over logs, through and around mucky areas, trekked through snow and climbed small rock ledges. Anna was twenty-five years Shannon's elder, nearly fifty-four, and carried a few extra pounds.

Anna took a pull from her water bottle and swiped her brow as she rested on the bench. She cleared her throat. "I should probably go to the gym I joined, huh?"

Shannon giggled.

Another rustling noise sounded close behind them. Shannon sprang to her feet and looked in its direction. "What caused that? It was the same noise I heard before, when we were by the water."

Anna shifted on the bench. "I don't know. I'm sure it was nothing," Anna replied as she slowly lifted herself from the bench. "We'd better get a move on. We've got a lot of ground to cover today."

As they proceeded down the trail toward the parking lot, Shannon glanced periodically over her shoulder.

"What's the matter? What do you keep looking for?" Anna asked.

Shannon hesitated before answering. After all she'd been through in the past three months, was she just being paranoid? She thought about her friends, Roland Hudson and Aaron Reed, murdered by a drug cartel last December at the mall while wearing their Santa and elf costumes. She thought about Tony Rosso, Chad Williams, Mike Carter and Joshua Meyers. Her past romantic interests all murdered last month on Valentine's Day while dressed as Cupid. With Saint Patrick's Day creeping up, she wasn't sure she could make it through another holiday. Especially since this one fell on her birthday—double whammy.

Shannon sighed. Was she really going to be twenty-eight in just two more days? She smiled at the thought of how happy it made her dad that she'd been born on Saint Patrick's Day. When she was younger, he'd always claimed the Saint Patrick's Day parades and festivities were thrown in celebration of her birthday. He'd been pretty convincing at the time. A vision of her dad's ear-to-ear smile played through her mind. She should pay her parents a visit soon. It had been a while.

The immediate issue at hand returned to Shannon. Could she make it through another holiday? She was running out of friends; hence, why she and Anna decided to take this geocaching trip. They wanted to get out of Milwaukee and harm's way.

Shannon met Anna's gaze. "I don't know. I feel like we're being watched."

Anna pointed at the patchy snow on the trail. "There aren't any footprints. I think the only things out here are birds, squirrels and maybe some deer.

Shannon looked ahead to the parking lot just in sight. *Thank God.* She threw one last glance over her shoulder. Nothing but trees swayed in the earthy-smelling breeze.

Shannon slid into the driver's seat of her blue Chevy Impala, cranked the engine, and threw the heater on full-blast as they headed in the direction of the next coordinates.

* * * *

Davin O'Brien leaned forward and dug the tips of his fingers into the cold brick ledge as he stood on his tiptoes. He watched Bernie Mathison through the large plate-glass window. Bernie tended to his customers as he cleaned up from the night before. It was early, not even 10:00 a.m. yet. A few old-timers sat at a table, playing cards, while they drank from coffee mugs. Several men sat on barstools that lined the long wooden bar, drinking what looked to be Bloody Marys with beer chasers.

Davin debated what to say to the lumberjack-like man who fit the recent description his father had given him. Why did Shannon O'Hara's uncle have to be so big? Of course, most everyone was big compared to Davin. Shaking his head in dismay, he wondered how on earth he would broach this topic. He had practiced the spiel his father had instructed him to use at least a thousand times in his head during his travels. Now suddenly, the pre-packaged words didn't seem appropriate. There was so much at stake, and his family counted on him. Davin swallowed the anxiety that rose in his throat. He couldn't fail them now, not when they needed him most.

Hardly able to keep his weary eyes open, let alone think, Davin glanced at his watch. He'd been up for nearly twenty-four hours already. Luckily, he had caught a catnap during his layover in Newark but it wasn't enough. Perhaps he should check into his hotel, get some rest and take care of business later. But time was of the essence.

He sighed, pulling his sweaty hands from the frosty ledge as he eased down from his tiptoe stance. His father's voice rang through his head. "I'm counting on you, son. You need to take care of this before it's too late. Our entire family depends on you. I know you'll do your best." For the first time, his father's voice was free of the condescending tone he normally used toward him. Why? Davin knew why. This time his almighty father found himself in a situation in which he desperately

5

needed his son. *Funny how that works.*

As Davin opened the door, the tiny bells on it clinked against the glass, drawing Bernie's attention. His shocked gaze was unmistakable. Bernie's torso deflated as the door shut, sucking the air from his lungs along with it. The large man's shoulders slumped as he pulled his hands from the dishwater and wiped them dry with a white terrycloth towel. He tossed the towel onto the counter and stepped toward the opening at the end of the long narrow bar.

Bernie's chest inflated and his dagger-shooting gaze darkened with each passing moment. Davin sucked in a breath and kept his eyes in check. *I guess he knows why I'm here.*

* * * *

Shannon parked the car. She and Anna slid out, eager and ready to embark on their second cache of the day.

Anna yanked at her jacket zipper. "Whoa, it's a bit nippier up here in the northern Door County peninsula."

"Windier too," Shannon added. She swiped her hair from in front of her eyes.

They planned to complete this cache and then drive back to Sturgeon Bay to join the rest of the contestants for the banquet at their hotel. She smiled to herself. In their rush to get up north, they nearly forgot to check in by the deadline as they buzzed through the city.

Shannon and Anna both glanced at the GPS unit. They plotted their hike with the use of the park's map given to them by the nice lady at the ranger station. They knew by the ranger's comments that they weren't the first team to arrive. They needed to hurry if they wanted to complete this cache before they lost daylight.

They started down the trail that would get them closest to the cache. The hike on the established trail would be about a mile or so but they weren't exactly sure the distance of the off-trail walk. The best they could figure at this point was an eighth of a mile, give or take a bit. But due to the lingering snow, even the walk on a well-used path would not be easy or quick.

The ladies chatted as they walked. Anna, as always, cut to the chase. "So how's it been going with that handsome Detective Spinelli of yours lately?"

Shannon glanced at her watch and then shot a smile over her shoulder. "Well, you took a bit longer than I expected," she teased.

Anna returned her smile. "I held out as long as I could. You know I'm living vicariously through you, so don't keep this old lady waiting here."

Shannon stopped and waited for Anna to catch up. "Actually, he's been kind of quiet and distant since the whole Valentine's Day episode. I can't seem to make him realize it wasn't his fault. Bethany had issues." Just saying Bethany's name sent a bone-chilling disturbance deep into her core.

Though the temperature still hovered around forty degrees, Anna swiped her gloved hand over her moist brow. "The poor guy. I'm not sure what to say. I can't imagine how it must feel to have a psycho ex-girlfriend kill four of his present girlfriend's ex-lovers, attempt to kill him and then kill herself. And on Valentine's Day of all days. The day I was sure he would pop the big question to you. What should have been one of the biggest and best days of his life turned out to be the worst."

"There's not a day goes by I don't think of that awful day. And he won't talk about it. The second I bring up the topic, he clams up." Shannon sighed. "And honestly, I really thought he would propose as well."

"With all that's gone on in the past three months, I'm surprised he let you out of his sight to come along on our girls' weekend."

"I know. I could tell by the look in his eyes when I told him our plans for this weekend, he wasn't pleased. He asked me to reconsider, but I couldn't. I really just needed to get away from the city and everything that has gone on lately. At first, he insisted upon coming along, but Captain Jackson assigned some hot case to him, Walker and Marsh. So he couldn't get away."

Shannon's eyes watered. Over the past three months, she'd found herself the happiest she'd ever been, the saddest, and the most frightened. She'd met Spinelli, and they'd gotten off to a rocky start. But she fell in love with him and couldn't be any happier, in regard to their relationship. During that same time frame, two of her co-workers had been murdered; she had been kidnapped and was next on the murder's

7

list. If Spinelli hadn't stepped in and saved the day, she would have been killed. The whole rescue was like something right out of a fairy tale with a knight in shining armor coming to the rescue of an endangered maiden. Truth be told, he was actually dressed in a Santa suit rather than armor. But that didn't matter to her; he was her knight no matter what he wore. And then of course, there was the issue with Spinelli's ex-girlfriend who sought a murderous revenge against the both of them. Again, Nick stepped in and saved the day. *My hero.*

Anna stepped forward and hugged Shannon. "I'm so sorry all this crap happened to you. You so didn't deserve any of this, but you can't change what's already happened. The only thing you can do is figure out how to deal with it and move forward."

"I know."

Shannon's cell phone vibrated. She pulled it from her zippered pocket and glanced at the display. She couldn't help but smile as she read the text from Spinelli.

Anna giggled. "What is that, number ten already?"

Shannon looked up and caught Anna's amused gaze. "Eight, but who's counting? Every hour on the hour." Though he went a bit overboard with the number of texts, Shannon—and the butterflies in her stomach—welcomed each and every one. His overprotectiveness warmed her heart. Like a schoolgirl, she desperately missed him already; they hadn't even been apart a full day.

Shannon shot off a quick response before she slipped her phone back into her pocket.

The ladies continued down the trail, Shannon leading the way. The wind picked up as they crossed over from the hardwoods to the cedars. The damp mossy smell let her know they neared the lake.

"Shannon."

"What?" Shannon asked as she looked over her shoulder.

Anna shrugged. "I didn't say anything."

"You didn't say my name?"

Anna pulled a frown. "No."

"Oh, hmm." Shannon would have sworn she'd heard someone say her name. She tried to shrug it off, tell herself it was just the wind, but the unease spiraling in the pit of her stomach forced her senses into 'full alert' mode.

Shannon forged on in the soft snow. Looking ahead, she could see the trail veered off to the north, just beyond the edge of the cedars where the hardwoods started again. Not much further to go.

A movement between the low-hanging branches of the cedar trees ahead caused Shannon to stop dead in her tracks. She squinted as if that would give her a better view.

Anna stepped next to her. "What's the matter? What are you looking at?"

Shannon kept her eyes focused ahead. "I thought I saw something move in that patch of trees ahead. Anna looked in that direction as well. The wind ceased as if someone flipped a switch. It was unusually still and quiet. *Eerie.*

Both women continued to stare forward for a few beats before Anna broke the silence. "I don't see anything. Maybe it was one of the other teams."

"The ranger said the two teams that checked in before us left already."

"Well, maybe it was a just a deer."

Anna was probably right. Deer tracks mingled among several sets of human footprints, but Shannon was unable to shrug off the cloak of apprehension. "Maybe."

Anna pulled her water bottle from her backpack, took a swig, and then put it back.

Shannon led onward. Her dry, wide-eyed gaze caused her eyes to itch but she refused to blink for fear of missing something. When they reached the end of the cedars where she'd seen the movement, she paused and looked around but found nothing unusual. A gust of wind blew by them. Whoosh … "Shannon."

Shannon spun to face Anna. "What?"

"I didn't say anything," Anna replied, her concerned gaze unmistakable. "Are you okay? You're as white as the snow."

Shannon swallowed down the anxiety rising in her throat. "I'm fine, just cold." Her voice shook but not nearly as much as her hands. She could hardly read the GPS.

Anna eyed her curiously before taking the GPS from her. She

studied the small screen for a moment and then pointed in the direction of the body of water lying just beyond the trees. "It shouldn't be too far from here."

They headed off-trail through the birch, maple and oak trees, following the footprints in the snow they assumed belonged to the other teams. The terrain was fairly flat until they came up upon a rock ledge, about Shannon's height. Shannon eased herself down the slick ledge, turned and watched Anna do the same. They followed the footprints to a pile of large downed trees that formed an equilateral triangle, hollowed on the inside. Shannon pulled herself up onto one of the logs and then slid down into the triangle to her waist. The square plastic cache container sat fully exposed in the center of the opening. She grabbed the container and set it on one of the logs between her and Anna.

Shannon slid the lever over and released the latch of the small cash drawer-like box before she lifted the lid. Both women gasped and jumped back, Shannon not as far as Anna as her back pressed firmly to the pine frame of the triangle. The box slipped off the log. The contents flipped through the air. Their horrifying screams echoed as Shannon's spine ground into the unyielding log behind her. Her gaze stayed glued to the gruesome object. *Oh God, please don't let it touch me!*

The container and its contents crashed to the ground and came to a rest at Shannon's feet. She wasted no time hoisting herself out of the confined area.

Shannon glanced over the downed trees to find her friend's equally petrified gaze on her. Speechless, Shannon waited for words from Anna.

Her friend swallowed audibly. "Is that what I think it is?"

Anna's shuddering body matched Shannon's own vibrations. The cold had nothing to do with it. Shannon's thudding heart nearly broke free of her chest.

"I think so."

Anna nodded at her and they both edged forward to get a better glimpse. A partially decomposed finger lay in the snow next to the cache box, along with the small broken jar in which it had been housed. A slight waft of alcohol drifted into Shannon's nostrils before a ray of sun shot through the overcast sky. A flash of light sparked off the finger. Shannon's heart raced. A gold Claddagh ring, just like the grand-prize she hoped to win, was wrapped snugly around the large yellowish-brown finger.

* * * *

Spinelli sat at his desk and scanned the financial records of one of the two murder victims found in downtown Milwaukee yesterday. Walker sat at the desk across from him doing the same with the other vic's records. Marsh sat off to the side, searching phone records. They'd been at it for hours and had come up empty.

Spinelli took a swig of his lukewarm coffee, set the mug back on its coaster and glanced around the precinct before he refocused his eyes on the vic's bank statement. The numbers blurred. He'd been at it too long. At this point, the evidence could jump off the page and bite him on the nose, and he probably wouldn't notice.

He propped his elbows on his desk, closed his eyes and rested his face in his hands. A vision of Shannon popped into his mind from hours earlier. Her pale body lay entwined among the mint green sheets on his bed. Bright red hair spilled like fire over his pillow. He recalled how her slow even breaths warmed the crook of his neck; how the soft curves of her body pressed up against him, nearly causing him to combust.

She looked so peaceful when she slept. He had hated the thought of waking her too early but the organ between his legs begged him to do so. They'd made love twice already but surely, one more time was in order, especially since he wouldn't see her for the remainder of the weekend.

Earlier in the day, he'd nearly begged her not to go on the Saint Patrick's Day weekend geocaching adventure. He sighed. He must have sounded like a desperate fool, but he just couldn't stand the thought of her being out of his sight with all that had gone on in the past several months. It nearly killed him that he couldn't go with her, but this double homicide just wouldn't allow for it.

Spinelli grunted in response to Walker's voice without even knowing what he said. He was selfish and knew it. He wanted to finish his reverie about Shannon before returning to the reality of the double homicide.

His body tensed at the mere memory of his and Shannon's most recent lovemaking session, when he'd lost his battle to lust and prematurely woke her earlier in the day. Her silky strands of hair washed over his face and chest as she crawled onto him. The sea of green that stared down at him whisked him away to some fantasyland where everything was pure, happy and satisfying. The Garden of Eden before the forbidden fruit was consumed.

Shannon had held his gaze as she guided him into her soft velvet opening. Lowering herself, she took in every bit of him. His hands, as if they had a mind of their own, flowed up her smooth stomach, not stopping until they cupped her small round breasts. Her breath hitched and her gaze intensified. She lifted upward then slowly eased down his shaft again. His hands tightened around her breasts before his thumb and forefinger found their way to her already taut nipples. He circled them before giving a delicate tug. Tossing her head back, a tantalizing groan escaped her plump red lips. Her small, warm hands slid over the top of his and urged him to continue. He didn't need urging. His pleasure grew tenfold at the sight, sound and feel of hers.

Spinelli recalled how Shannon's pumping increased as his hands roamed her welcoming body. Blood rushed through his veins at the speed of light. He knew if she kept that pace, he wouldn't last too long. His hands drifted down from her breasts, skimming her soft, warm skin until one came to rest on her hip, and the other at her sensitive, swollen bead. Pressing his thumb against it, he was saved. It didn't take long for her walls to clamp around him, milking him for all he was worth. His body tensed one last time before he spilled himself into her.

Shannon floated forward with the grace of an angel, until the soft curves of her breasts pressed firmly to his chest. Her warm cheek rested against his. The silky strands of her hair clung to his face and shoulder. He inhaled deeply. Her sweet scent reminded him of a fresh spring morning. He wrapped his arms around her, thinking he should really stake his claim. He loved her and he wanted her to be his forever.

The beating of her heart matched his. He thought about the ring tucked away in his dresser drawer. He'd nearly popped the question just over a month ago, on Valentine's Day, but the events of the day precluded him from doing so. Assuming she'd say yes, he didn't want her to associate the day of their engagement with the same day his psycho ex-girlfriend killed four of Shannon's past love interests. Just over a month had passed since that awful day, and he still hadn't asked her to marry him. He wasn't sure why; he definitely wanted to. Her birthday was coming up, perhaps that would be a good time to ask her to become his wife.

Walker cleared his throat and snapped Spinelli out of his daydream.

He lifted his head from his hands and caught Walker's gaze. "What?"

"What the heck? Were you sleeping? Your phone's been ringing."

Spinelli grabbed his cellphone from his hip and glanced at the display screen. Shannon's green-eyed gaze stared back at him. A wave of excitement washed through him with the force of a tidal wave. He tapped the screen and placed the phone to his ear. "Hi sweetheart. How's it going?"

Shannon gasped in response.

Spinelli's heart leaped into his throat. "Shannon, what's wrong? Are you okay?"

She gasped again.

"Shannon, sweetheart, what is it?"

Detectives Walker and Marsh's gazes were now on him.

"A finger, Nick, we found a finger in the cache container."

"What?"

Spinelli heard Shannon suck in another quick breath, and though he could hear Anna in the background, he couldn't make out what she said.

He knew by the anxiety in both Shannon and Anna's voice that the finger was real and not some sort of prank to go along with the cache game. A boatload of questions flooded his mind. Why was there a finger in the container and what did it have to do with Shannon and Anna? And were they in real danger? Spinelli fought for a controlled voice. "Shannon, sweetheart, calm down and tell me exactly what happened and where you are."

"We're at the second cache of the day in Newport State Park. We found a finger in the cache box and it's wearing a gold Claddagh ring. And to make matters worse, I feel like someone has been following us all day."

Spinelli's heart slammed against his ribcage nearly knocking him over. Even though his instincts had already informed him of the danger, hearing her speak of a stalker confirmed his nightmare as reality.

"Have you called the authorities?"

"Anna's on the phone with them right—"

A horrifying scream penetrated Spinelli's ear before the call disconnected. His heart plummeted into his stomach. Walker and Marsh leapt to their feet and narrowed the gap between them, all staring at the phone in Spinelli's hand.

Spinelli tapped the screen. Shannon's cell went to voicemail. Anna's did the same.

Chapter Two

Captain Jackson hung up the phone receiver and met Spinelli's gaze. "The sheriff's deputy is en route to the park and the park ranger is hiking to Shannon and Anna's last known location. She'll continue to try their cells but says the odds of getting through are pretty slim since there's very little reception in the park. Quite frankly, she was surprised they were able to reach you and 911 in the first place."

"How long will it take them to get there?"

"The ranger should be on location in about five or ten minutes. The deputy will be at the park entrance in five but then he's got to hike in as well."

Spinelli sank into his chair. A lot could happen in that time frame, and he had no clue as to what had happened already. His mind reeled. "Did she say anything about the finger?"

"The ranger is a bit confused about that. She said she spoke to both of the other teams as they exited the park and they didn't mention anything about a finger being in the cache. As far as she knew no one else visited the park today, at least not through the main entrance, but it is a big park."

"Is she the only ranger working today?"

"Yes. Evidently, there isn't much activity at the park this time of year. It's a good thing she actually lives on the grounds."

Spinelli stared down at his phone and willed it to ring. Shannon's sparkling emerald green eyes stared back at him. Her plump, ruby red lips turned up in a soft smile. He loved her smile and soft kissable lips that always seemed to meld perfectly to his. He drew in a slow deep breath to calm his racing heart. It didn't work. His memory unleashed

Shannon's sweet tantalizing scent and snuffed out the bitter coffee odor that permeated the walls of the precinct. Though he'd set her photo as his phone's wallpaper months ago, he still found himself pulling out his cell several times a day just to look at her. He couldn't seem to help himself, he loved her. That wholesome smile reminded him of the goodness this world had to offer. Conversely, the clientele he often encountered through his work reminded him of just the opposite: the bad, the evil and the cold, hard cruelty that existed in the world. Her lovely photo had become a crutch to get him through the hard days.

He blew out a sigh. *After all that's gone on in the past several months, why in the hell did I let her out of my sight?*

He tore his gaze from his phone and met Jackson's concerned stare as he absently placed the phone back in its holder on his hip. Jackson's dark-eyed gaze was unusually soft. He'd seen that gentle look from her only a couple of times before, both times being incidents that involved him and Shannon. He liked Captain Jackson. She was tough but honest and fair. Her small frame never precluded her from getting the difficult jobs done; her twenty plus years on the force had taught her how to appropriately handle nearly any situation.

Walker and Marsh pushed their way through Jackson's door. Walker took a seat in the chair next to Spinelli and Marsh planted himself on the credenza behind Jackson's desk.

"Well?" Jackson asked. Her inquisitive gaze looked as though it was pinning Walker to his chair.

"I just talked with the Chief Deputy of Door County. They contacted the cache game organizers and put a halt to the game. Now they're assembling the teams at the Justice Center for interviews and collecting all the caches. Due to the close proximity of the resort to the Justice Center, it should only take them a few minutes to get everyone together. They'll call when they know more." Walker shifted his gaze to the floor and tugged at a string hanging from his cuff.

Jackson's glare stayed on him. "Is there more?"

It didn't surprise Spinelli one bit that she seemed to know Walker withheld some information.

Walker shifted in his seat and hesitantly lifted his gaze to meet Jackson's. "The Chief Deputy reminded me that Door County is not our jurisdiction. As of right now, there's no proof of any crime or wrong-doing."

Deep down Spinelli knew the Chief Deputy was right, but he hadn't heard Shannon's blood-curdling scream as her cell cut out. Spinelli intentionally avoided Jackson's gaze. If he looked at her, she'd know exactly what he was thinking.

"Spinelli."

He glanced at Walker for support before meeting Jackson's gaze.

"No, Spinelli. I know what you are thinking and no, you may not," Jackson said, reading his mind as clearly as if it was her own. "Let's give the Door County Sheriff's Department a few minutes to figure out what's going on, and then we'll take it from there." Walker offered no support. They both knew Jackson was right. He couldn't just hop in his car and drive to Door County. Oh, how he wanted to, but he couldn't. First off, if Shannon was truly missing, the Door County Sheriff's department would likely treat him as a 'Person of Interest', and they'd prevent him from helping with the case. He knew the drill. He'd seen it and done it enough times.

Spinelli leaned back in his chair, closed his eyes and massaged his temples. The throbbing remained. *What happened? Why did she scream like that? Where is she?*

* * * *

Spinelli returned to his desk and the financial records of the murder victim he'd been working on earlier in the day. Walker was at his desk doing the same with the other vic's records. Marsh resumed scanning the phone records. They were back to business as usual, as if he hadn't received a distress call from Shannon.

The documents before him turned into one blurry mass. He pinched the bridge of his nose between his thumb and forefinger as he squeezed his eyes shut, hoping to clear his vision. It didn't work. His vision and concentration failed him. He couldn't make sense of anything on the papers before him.

He glanced up at Walker and caught his pinning gaze. It didn't take a rocket scientist to know that Jackson had tasked Walker with keeping an eye on him. Jackson knew him too well; he'd make a run for it if given the opportunity. Though he knew he could garner empathy from Walker, he'd have a better chance at getting Marsh to assist in an escape.

Spinelli rose from his chair.

Walker zoned in on him and sprang to his feet. "Where are you going?"

Spinelli ground his teeth together and glared at his friend. He felt like a caged animal. "Bathroom." He didn't care if he just lied to his friend or stretched the truth. He was going to go to the bathroom but in all reality, if given an opening, he'd be out the door.

He stepped out of the restroom to find Walker leaned against the wall waiting for him.

"Really?"

Walker sighed.

Spinelli returned to his desk and dialed both Shannon and Anna's cell numbers as he'd done countless times in the past couple hours. Both immediately went to voicemail. *Would Walker and Jackson just leave already? It's Friday night for crissake. They never stay this late, especially Jackson.*

Every time he glanced through the Captain's office window, she was on the phone, talking to the Door County Sheriff's Department he assumed.

Spinelli's desk phone rang and Jackson's number flashed across the display screen. "Hello."

"Grab Walker and Marsh and come in here," she said, leaving him unable to read anything in her tone.

Spinelli stood and motioned for Walker and Marsh to follow him.

They crammed into Jackson's small office.

Jackson looked up from her computer screen. "I just hung up with the Chief Deputy. They've found nothing but legitimate caches at each location, including the Newport site where Shannon and Anna were last. No signs of struggle, nothing. They've also touched base with the other players but nothing else unusual has happened."

"Dammit! What in the hell?" Spinelli yelled.

Jackson shook her head. "I don't know. All seems normal with the exception of Shannon's phone call to you, and Anna's to 911. Yet there's no sign of them or Shannon's car at the park."

Spinelli glanced at Walker and knew they were of a like mind. Though they knew the truth, no concrete evidence had been found to indicate that the ladies were truly missing. In all likelihood, the Sheriff's Department would not allocate more resources until something else turned up.

Spinelli sprang out of his chair. Walker leaped to his feet in response.

"I'll drive." Marsh chimed in.

Jackson's gaze shifted between them, a tinge of regret evident in her eyes. He knew she wished she had let him leave earlier. "I'll take a burger and fries," she responded, unwilling to verbally acknowledge their plan. As the party in charge, it was her job to follow the rules; Spinelli knew that. The evidence was such he understood her earlier decision, though he didn't like it.

Within the hour, Marsh pulled into Spinelli's driveway with Walker already in the car. The drive on 43 North toward Door County would take nearly three hours. At least this time of year there would be no traffic to hold them up. But still, three long hours. A lot could happen— or not happen--in three hours. Was she simply lost? Scared? His breath caught in his throat. Or had she really been abducted? Was she waiting for him to rescue her? *Dammit, why didn't I leave when she first called? Hours—valuable time--lost.* Sweat beaded on his upper lip and brow. He swallowed hard as he imagined the worst. Was she hurt? Or worse, was she...*No.* Even silently, he couldn't finish that last question. His heart couldn't take it, and his mind wouldn't bear the thought.

Spinelli tapped the screen of his cellphone for the tenth time in the past hour. Perhaps she'd answer this time. No luck.

Marsh flipped on his turn signal.

"What are you doing?" Spinelli asked, unable to keep the frustration from his tone.

Marsh glanced at him through the rearview mirror. "I have to take a whiz."

"For crissake, can't you hold it?"

"We need gas, too," Marsh replied as he pulled up to the pump.

"Fine then, go whiz while I pump the gas," Spinelli replied.

Back on the road, Spinelli tapped his phone screen again. Same result.

He raked his hand over his face. Shannon's scream and disconnected call was not enough to allow for formally contacting her cell phone provider to ping her phone for a location. He'd have to wait until the circumstances substantiated such a request. A sharp pain shot through his chest. He might not make it through the agonizing period.

Marsh parked the car in the lot of the Sturgeon Bay resort and conference center where the geocachers were booked. On one hand, Spinelli was relieved to see only a few cars in the parking lot; they'd likely have rooms available for them. On the other hand, the scarceness of vehicles made it easy to see that Shannon's Impala was nowhere to be found.

Spinelli grabbed his duffle bag, slung it over his shoulder and headed toward the front doors of the dimly lit hotel with Walker and Marsh in tow. Cool air swirled off the partially frozen bay and nipped at Spinelli's face. He hadn't expected it to be quite so cold yet in the middle of March, but then he recalled TV weather reports about the unusual weather in Door County. Other than the whistling wind, all was quiet. None of the usual city noises Spinelli was accustomed to: no sirens, horns or screeching tires, and no shouts of profanity on the street.

Walker scooted ahead and opened the door. A blast of heat washed over Spinelli as he stepped through the doorway. A large stone fireplace stood in the corner of the open concept reception area. Gas flames roared. A young lady sat alone on an over-sized leather couch near the fire. Her eyes stayed fixed on the screen of her laptop as her fingers danced over the keyboard. Marsh hit the bell for service at the unmanned reception counter just beyond the couch. A large ship-wheel clock hung above the desk. It read 10:30. They'd made pretty good time.

Faint laughter echoed from the wide hall that spilled into the reception area. Spinelli's heart sank. He didn't recognize any of the laughter as he hoped he would. But in that split-second, his heart begged him to look down the hall anyway before his logical brain took over. She wasn't there. His gaze drifted to the large brown sign on the wall engraved with 'Bar' and 'Conference Center'. An arrow pointed down the hall.

Marsh grabbed Spinelli and Walker's duffle bags from them. "I'll ditch these in the rooms and meet you guys at the bar. And no, the receptionist wouldn't give me Shannon and Anna's room number but she called it and no one answered."

Marsh knew him too well. Spinelli wouldn't be able to rest and start his investigation in the morning. He would head to the bar, question the clientele from the geocaching game and find out if they knew anything about Shannon and Anna.

Spinelli and Walker took a seat at the retro-modern bar and ordered some drafts. The young female bartender immediately fixed her intense blue-eyed gaze on Spinelli. Months ago, before he and Shannon started dating, he would have not only eaten up her attention but likely worked to intensify it. Now he just needed information from her. Nothing more.

The room, fairly empty with the tourist season over, held mostly female patrons. Spinelli assumed they were geocachers. They'd sit and listen for a while, and see if they had any information that would help find Shannon and Anna.

Marsh pulled up a stool next to Spinelli. The bartender came over to get his order but kept her gaze on Spinelli. She spun on her heel and sashayed to the taps, returning a moment later with Marsh's frosty mug in hand. Easy target.

"Where are you all from?" she asked, though her gaze never left Spinelli.

"Milwaukee."

"Up here for business or pleasure?"

Spinelli forced his lady-killer smile and worked to darken his gaze. The very gaze Shannon's friend Anna often teased could talk a woman into anything without a word being spoken. Both would surely work on the bartender, she was a talker. If she had any information he needed, it wouldn't take much to get it out of her. "A little of both."

"I'm Corrina," she said as she extended her hand toward him.

"Nice to meet you. I'm Nick." He gestured toward Marsh. "This is Greg," he said and then gestured toward Walker. "This is Brad." Their first names sounded strange on his tongue. He couldn't remember if he'd ever called them by their first names before.

Corrina shook each man's hand before her welcoming gaze returned to Spinelli. She reached toward him and rested her hand on his forearm.

"Are you here to work at the shipyard?" Hmm, she naturally assumed he was a physical laborer. Evidently, his workouts were paying off.

Before he could answer her question, a lady at the curve of the bar—just on the other side of Marsh—motioned for Corrina.

Corrina padded off to mix the lady's drink.

Marsh leaned forward and peeked around Spinelli. "Hey, Walker, you think she even knows we're here?"

Walker chuckled. It was business as usual. All the ladies gravitated toward Spinelli.

They sucked down the last of their second beer and decided to call it a night. They'd only gathered old information from Corrina. The women from the geocaching weekend adventure were all at this resort but the game had resumed play after the initial scare with Shannon and Anna. Yet Shannon and Anna were still nowhere to be found. The other participants assumed Shannon and Anna had simply called it quits due to the uncooperative, cold weather.

* * * *

Davin rubbed his sweaty palms together as he paced his large, dark hotel suite. He needed to call his father and get him up to speed about his conversation with Shannon's Uncle Bernie. A multitude of excuses to avoid the dreaded call flashed through his mind.

Davin glanced at the clock. Almost midnight, which meant it was nearly 6:00 a.m. in Ireland. His dad probably already waited by the phone for his call. Why did his dad always get up so early? He didn't have to work. He'd never worked a day in his life, living off old family money. The same pot of money Davin wanted to secure. He blew out an exaggerated breath in recognition of his previous failed efforts.

A sweet fragrance lingered from the open bottle of Jameson on the bedside table. It crept through the darkness and teased Davin's nostrils. His mouth watered at the thought of another swallow of the robust, yet smooth, nectar. Perhaps just one more glass could calm his nerves. He tossed his two-drink limit out the window.

Traditional Irish dance music blared from the desk in the corner of the suite, and the light from his cellphone lit up the dark room. Davin knew his father would be on the other end of the line. Perhaps if he ignored it, his father would think he was still sleeping; after all, it was only midnight here in Wisconsin. *Wisconsin, seriously?* He never would have thought in a million years that he'd visit Wisconsin. The United States he could have imagined but Wisconsin, the land of dairy cows?

The music stopped, but Davin knew it would only be a matter of time before it started up again.

Even though he knew sleep wouldn't come, he climbed up onto the bed anyhow. He flipped on the reading lamp and snatched up the photo of Shannon he had placed on the nightstand. He eyed the photo and wondered how his father had come to acquire the recent picture of Ms. O'Hara. Davin held the picture closer to his eyes. She was a thing of beauty with milky white skin, bright shiny red hair and piercing emerald-green eyes. A man could easily lose himself in those eyes. Davin supposed Spinelli did. He thought about how he would handle Spinelli if the need arose. The cop's reputation preceded him.

Davin switched the light off and lay back on the bed with Shannon's photo pressed between his hand and his heart. He felt sorry for her. She didn't deserve this. He sighed heavily. A deal was a deal, and their grandfathers had shaken on it. What had Emmet O'Brien and Winston Mathison been thinking when they'd made such an agreement? Shannon's grandfather, Winston, had died more than forty-five years ago. Yet Davin's own grandfather, Emmet, insisted the Mathison family make good on the deal struck between the two men nearly sixty years ago. *Crazy dying bastard.* Davin never much cared for his Grandpa O'Brien; he was a wicked old tyrant. He cared for him even less now. But his family counted on him to secure the old family fortune before his eighty-eight year old grandfather passed. He needed to prove to his own father, once and for all, that he was worthy of the O'Brien name.

* * * *

Shannon opened her eyes to a pitch-black room. Her dry throat itched. She swallowed and ran her tongue over her teeth. *What is that awful metallic taste?* Her tongue gravitated to her teeth again; the taste grew stronger. When she inhaled, her eyes instantly watered like she'd just inhaled flames. Her right hand moved toward her nose but jerked to a halt inches from her face. *What the heck?* She tried to move her hand closer to her face but it wouldn't budge. With her other hand, she came across a thin rope wrapped around her wrist. The opposite end was fastened to the bedpost.

A low groan echoed in the blackness. Shannon sprang off the bed nearly jerking her shoulder out of its socket. The small length of rope didn't let her go too far. Another breathy moan penetrated the incredibly thick air. Shannon fumbled around the nightstand next to the bed for a lamp. She nearly knocked it over before she located the toggle switch at the base. The now dimly lit room allowed her to focus on the body in the bed. It was Anna. Her left wrist was bound to the bedpost on the opposite side of the bed.

Sheer panic ripped through her. Where were they? How did they end up here? And who tied them to the bed?

Shannon climbed back onto the bed and shook her friend's shoulder. "Anna, wake up."

Anna stirred but her eyes remained closed.

She glanced around the room for something within reach to cut the rope. A small glass-top table with two leather chairs facing a stone fireplace sat in the corner of the room. To the left of the fireplace were a desk and chest of drawers with a TV centered on the top. Even if there had been something of use on any of the furniture, she couldn't reach it.

Oddly, the room resembled the hotel room she and Anna had rented for the geocaching adventure, only larger and nicer. A suite? Shannon looked for a way out. To her left was a hallway, presumably leading to the bathroom. She assumed the door directly in front of her led to an adjoining room, perhaps the room of her captor. If she and Anna wanted to escape, they had better hurry. She had no idea how they wound up in this room but she needed out.

Shannon swallowed hard. The metallic taste faded, and with each breath, her nostrils stung a bit less. *It's like they've been burnt raw.*

After another quick glance around the room, Shannon leaned closer to Anna's face. "Anna, wake up. We need to go," she whispered softly, fearing her captors might hear her.

Anna's eyes fluttered open. Her confused gaze zoned in on Shannon. "What?"

"We gotta go," Shannon replied as she worked to free her bound wrist from the bedpost.

Anna sat up and glanced at her own roped limb. She spun at the waist and faced Shannon again. "What in the world is going on?"

"Shh, I don't know. Just get yourself untied and let's get out of here. Shannon freed her wrist and then worked on Anna's. The older woman sucked in a breath and expelled it. "Holy man, my nose feels like I inhaled sulfur or something. It tastes like someone poured acid in my mouth."

"Yeah, mine too, but it's wearing off."

The women slid off the bed and scoped the room for a phone and an exit. No phone. And as for exits, their only two options seemed to be the sliding glass doors leading to the balcony or the door to the adjoining room.

Shannon parted the vertical blinds that covered the sliding glass doors and gripped the handle. A rush of cool damp air played havoc on her still tender nostrils. They stepped onto the balcony and around a small patio set to assess their surroundings. The balcony faced another wing of the hotel. Though viewing the building from a different angle, Shannon knew this was the same hotel she and Anna checked into earlier in the day. Not one single room opposite them glowed with light. Perhaps the hotel didn't use that wing during off-season. She leaned over the rail and craned her head to the right to find a dim glow of streetlights off in the distance. To the left she found the bay of water, just a couple hundred yards away. Residential lights shined sporadically across the bay. At that distance, a yell for help would likely go unanswered. She counted the levels beneath them. Three floors up. Jumping was not an option.

She had no idea of the time but the black starless sky clearly indicated they'd been out for quite a while. The last time Shannon could note was 3:30 p.m. or so, when they discovered the finger in the cache box. A shiver penetrated her body either from the cold or the recollection of the severed finger.

They retreated into the room and assessed their only option. Shannon pressed her ear to the adjoining-room door. Nothing, not even the glow of a light beneath it. She dropped to her knees and pressed her cheek to the floor anyway to take a look. Nothing. She sprang back to her feet and shook her head. "It's pitch black. I can't see anything," she whispered.

Anna nodded. Wrapping her hand around the knob, Shannon turned it slowly and gave a slight pull. The near-dark adjoining room felt eerily still. A faint glow peeked out from the crack under the door directly across the main room they now entered. It gave her enough light to make out the kitchenette to the left and the living room area to the right. Yep, they were in a hotel suite and she could only assume their captor occupied the other adjoining room from which the light came.

Shannon tiptoed toward the kitchenette, hoping to find an exit. Anna was on her heels. She worked her way around the kitchen counter, praying there would be an exit around the corner.

The stench of whiskey assaulted her sensitive nostrils. Her eyes had adjusted enough to the darkness to make out a couple booze bottles laying sideways on the countertop. The bottle caps lay next to them. *For crying out loud, did we sleep through a party? More importantly, how in the world did we come to be here?* Shannon shook her head. She'd worry about that later, when they were safely away from here.

Once in the narrow aisle between the kitchen appliances and the kitchen bar, Shannon noticed a faint crack on the floor. A hall door. Relief rippled through her, they were nearly home free.

Shannon halted at the presence in front of her. She squinted. There was nothing visible between her and the door yet she couldn't seem to get her feet to move forward. She edged back, bumping into Anna.

"What's the matter?" Anna whispered.

"I don't know. It just doesn't feel right to move forward."

Anna grabbed Shannon's hand. "I want to get the heck out of here," she blurted as she scooted around Shannon and lunged for the door, attempting to tug Shannon along with her. Shannon dug her heels in.

A crackling sound hissed as a lightning bolt flared in front of them; fog as thick as pea soup filled the suite.

A metallic taste clung to Shannon's tongue as if she'd just licked the floor of a machine shop. Fire ripped through her nostrils. Anna fell back onto her and they tumbled to the ground. Shannon's mind reeled. She couldn't see, couldn't speak. The air drained from her lungs.

* * * *

Spinelli propped himself up on his elbow and used his fist to hammer his pillow in place. Why he even bothered to attempt to sleep was beyond him. Through the slit in the vertical blinds, he could see it was still dark outside. The clock read 3:00 a.m. He grabbed his phone off the nightstand for the hundredth time since he'd climbed into bed. Still no call from Shannon. His chest constricted, nearly enough to squelch his beating heart.

Marsh's thunderous snores reverberated through the paper-thin walls of the hotel. Spinelli wondered if Walker could hear him across the hall as well.

Spinelli buried his head between two pillows. It didn't help. *For crissake, would he just stop already?* He flung the covers back, rolled out of bed and stomped off to the bathroom.

He glared at his reflection in the mirror and wondered why in the hell he'd let Shannon traipse off on this geocaching weekend without him. After all that had happened to her and around her in the past several months, he should have known better.

Spinelli tore his gaze from the accusatory reflection. He reached over to turn on the faucet before he leaned forward, cupped his hands and splashed his hot face with cool water. The hotel spared no heat, nearly cooking him out of his room. He turned off the water and buried his face in a towel. A faint crackling noise captured his attention. It reminded him of a Fourth of July sparkler. He looked about the tiny bathroom for the source of the noise. Within seconds, the sound disappeared. Perhaps it had come from the drain.

He spun on his heel, flipped off the light and stepped out of the bathroom to be greeted by a sharp sulfuric scent that left just as quickly as it came. The slight burning sensation in his nostrils substantiated the fact he hadn't imagined the smell. His eyelids grew heavy. He welcomed the yawn that followed but not the lightheadedness that accompanied it. Perhaps he had a shot at a couple hours of shut-eye, and he'd feel better when he woke up.

Spinelli's throbbing head woke him. When it ceased, he rolled over and nearly fell off the bed. How in the hell did he end up at the foot of the bed? Flipping over, he remembered he'd gone to the bathroom in the wee morning hours. His itchy nose reminded him of the strange odor as he exited the bathroom. A hint of a metallic flavor still coated his tongue.

The pounding resumed. "Spinelli, are you up?" Walker's muffled voice sounded through the door.

Spinelli sat up. He glanced at the clock. It was 5:05 a.m.

"Spinelli," Walker yelled through the door again.

"Yeah, just a second," he replied as he slid into a pair of jeans.

He pulled the door open to find both Walker and Marsh in the hall.

"You look like death warmed over. Are you feeling okay?" Marsh asked, never one for sugar coating anything. Was that Marsh's version of delicate? If things weren't so grim in regard to Shannon, Spinelli probably would have laughed...

"I'm fine. I didn't get much sleep last night. I didn't fall asleep until after 3:00, but then I seemed to crash really hard.

"Hmm, 3:00. That was right around the time a weird crackling noise woke me up," Walker stated.

"You heard that too?"

"Yeah, it fizzed in and out really quick. At first I thought I had dreamt it, but then I smelled something acidy and then rotten eggs. It actually made my nose burn for a bit. I half expected the fire alarms to go off. I even got up and checked the hallway."

"And what about that awful taste?" Spinelli asked.

Walker cocked a brow. "What taste?"

"That metallic flavor."

Walker shook his head.

"What in the hell are you guys talking about? I didn't hear, smell or taste anything," Marsh cut in.

"Quite frankly, I'm surprised we could hear anything over you sawing down that forty acre forest last night. For crying out loud, do you have sleep apnea or what?" Walker asked Marsh.

"I don't snore that loud."

Walker rolled his eyes before Spinelli cut off their banter. "I was in the bathroom when it happened and thought it came from the drain."

Walker shrugged.

Marsh's stomach growled nearly as loud as his snoring.

His gaze shifted between Spinelli and Walker. "I can't help it. I woke up starving."

"Well, you did work hard in the woods last night," Walker joked.

Marsh opened his mouth to reply but Spinelli cut him off. "I'm gonna shower quick and then I'll meet you guys downstairs in the restaurant. Just order something for me so it's ready when I get there. Then we can get a move on."

Spinelli shaved and showered, slapped on some clothes and then headed to the hotel restaurant to meet Walker and Marsh.

He'd just finished his short stack of pancakes and sausage when the waitress delivered not only the bill but a large sealed envelope as well.

"What's this about?" Spinelli asked as he took the envelope from the waitress who'd also fixed her curious gaze on the envelope.

She shrugged. "I don't know. Some guy just came in, pointed at you and asked that I deliver it. Then he left."

All heads snapped in the direction of the doorway. Spinelli sprang to his feet and headed for the doorway, Walker and Marsh on his heels. Other than the receptionist, the lobby was empty. They stepped into the parking lot. No movement. There didn't appear to be any activity up or down the street either, but the slow breaking daylight made it difficult to see very far.

The frigid air forced them back inside the building. Spinelli stared at the envelope in his hand. His gut told him the contents weren't good but he still needed to check.

Spinelli opened the seal. Anguish exploded in his core and seeped through his veins as he scanned the paperwork. The grapefruit sized lump in his throat cut off his oxygen supply. Unable to speak, he just stared at the document as Walker and Marsh's words became muffled. The paper floated to the floor.

Chapter Three

Shannon's eyes popped opened to the same dark room. *How in the heck did I end up back here and back in this bed?* She inhaled. Her burning nostrils unleashed her most recent memory. She and Anna had snuck through the dark suite to escape whomever. She recalled the strange hiss, the bright light and the fog. The fading metallic taste on her tongue had become part of an unpleasant routine. Shannon sighed. They'd been so close to an escape.

It surprised her to find her wrist bound to the headboard of the bed; tied in the same manner as before. Wouldn't her captor know she and Anna would just untie themselves like last time? It took only a moment for realization to sink into her foggy brain. The air drained from her lungs. He was watching them. The rope, meant as an inconvenience, would only slow them down if they tried to escape again.

Shannon scanned the darkened suite for a video camera, but she could hardly make out the furniture, let alone a small camera. And fear of her captor seeing her and Anna kept her from flipping on the light.

Shannon turned her head to the side to check on Anna. Sheer panic shot through her veins, rocking her body at the sight of the empty spot beside her. Tears flooded her eyes. It was bad enough before when she at least had Anna. Now, to make matters worse, she was on her own. *Anna, where are you?* Knowing Anna would never leave her side during a time like this, she could only assume the worst.

The urge to sob was nearly uncontrollable. Shannon swallowed hard to suppress the cries about to escape her dry throat. If her captor was watching, she didn't want him to know she was awake. She needed time to think. *What does he want from me? Maybe I should scream.*

30

If she had just listened to Nick, this wouldn't be happening. He had pleaded with her not to take this trip, especially since he couldn't accompany her. He wasn't the begging type but evidently, in his gut, he knew something bad would happen.

Shannon's pulse pounded in her ears. Why didn't she trust his instincts? She was such a fool. What she'd give to be in his large warm bed wrapped in his strong arms, pressed against that hard-muscled body and inhaling his manly woodsy scent rather than alone and afraid in this strange bed.

Shannon recalled the flash of concern, followed by the boyishly sad look in his charcoal eyes as she refused his plea to stay home this weekend. Tears saturated her pillow. What had she done to deserve this? After all that had gone on in the past three months, now Anna? Outside of her immediate family, all she had left was Anna and Nick. If she believed in reincarnation, surely she must have been some sort of wickedly cruel person in a previous life to deserve what had happened to her lately.

Shannon's mind scrambled to come up with a logical explanation for her incarceration. Who would have a reason to do such a thing to her? More importantly, what were their plans for her? Were they going to kill her, rape her? At present, they hadn't really harmed her. Or were they really after Anna? Shannon decided to hope for the best. Maybe another team temporarily taking them out of commission so they could win the grand prize? Yeah, she and Anna would be miraculously released after the game. Even though she should be angry, Shannon sighed with relief at the thought of this best-case scenario. Then reality punched her in the gut. Her pulse quickened. If it were that simple, why wasn't Anna with her right now? The mind is a wonderful but scary thing. It's amazing what it can talk a person into at times.

Shannon racked her brain, trying to come up with anyone who would do this to her. In her line of work, it wasn't uncommon to make enemies. During her nearly four years as a social worker, she'd become the 'caseworker of record' for numerous families. Oh, how she hated the term 'caseworker of record.' It sounded so unconceivably cold and formal, especially when the attorneys used the phrase during examination on the witness stand. In her short time as a caseworker, she must have been asked the same question at least a thousand times, "Ms. O'Hara, you've been the caseworker of record for **insert name** for how long?" She could tell her clientele despised that question as well. Especially when the timeframe in which she worked with the family spanned over a couple of years. Such a period of time wasn't all that uncommon, but it really looked bad for the clientele. In many cases, it meant they were not making much progress, or progressing quickly enough.

As she thought about one of the most recent times she had been asked that hateful routine question, Lamar and Chandra Clarkson came to mind. Her testimony that day had prevented the Clarkson's from getting their children back. The Clarkson's had been arrested for habitually dealing marijuana. Their two young children had been placed in foster care for several months prior to the hearing last December. After the school psychologist and Shannon's testimonies, it looked evident that the Clarkson's would not regain custody of their children. Like many other cases, Mr. Clarkson had not completed the recommended rehabilitation program, nor had the Clarkson's made any effort to undergo the suggested counseling. Lately, Shannon couldn't help but feel she just wasted her breath to recommend rehabilitation and counseling to the clientele. She'd find herself in court, months later, testifying on the children's behalf instead of the parents who never seemed to take her recommendations.

Shannon blew out an exaggerated breath. As long as she lived, she would never forget that day in the courtroom with the Clarkson's. There had been such wrath on Lamar's face, as she testified to recommend continued foster care for the kids. She'd been dismissed from the witness chair and headed back to her seat behind the children's attorney. The gratified look in the children's attorney's eyes reassured her she'd done well on the stand.

As she walked by the Clarkson's court-appointed attorney, she shot him a quick glance. A look of contentment nestled in his eyes. Unable to help herself, she eyed the Clarksons for a split-second. Lamar leapt from his chair and attacked her. As they tumbled to the ground, she hit her head on the railing behind the attorney tables. A kaleidoscope of fireworks flashed in her eyes, her teeth rattled and her head rang like church bells. 'Rang like church bells,' a saying passed down from her diehard Catholic grandmother to her mother, and now to her. She'd heard her mother use the phrase more than she could count, but it really seemed to fit at that point in time. What she would give right now to hear her mother's voice recite the expression again. It had taken hours for the ringing in her head to stop and a couple of days for her headache to disappear altogether.

Could someone like Lamar Clarkson, or one of the many others she'd crossed through the years, have done this to her? Possibly, but she couldn't imagine they'd go through the effort of following her all the way to Door County from Milwaukee. His kind would probably just wait in a dark parking lot or march into her office and do what they wanted to her.

Shannon huffed. She wasn't about to wait around any longer and run these useless scenarios through her head. *Screw it!* "Help me, someone please help me!" Shannon yelled at the top of her lungs. Knowing her soft voice wouldn't carry far, she gave it her best shot. About to yell again, she was startled by the creak of the adjoining door, followed by light that suddenly illuminated the room. Her eyes quickly shifted to the door, only to catch a glimpse of a small childlike hand retreating through the crack in the doorway.

The door remained ajar. A brief moment of silence filled the air. Shannon waited.

"You'll keep your mouth shut and stay put if you know what's good for your friend," an unusually high-pitched male voice commanded.

The lump in Shannon's throat nearly choked her. "Anna?" she squeaked inadvertently.

"Yes, Anna. If all goes according to plan today, your friend will be released unharmed."

Plan, what plan?

The door closed. The light remained on. Shannon scooted into a sitting position on the bed and pressed her back against the headboard. She pulled her knees to her chest and wrapped her arms around her quivering legs. The rope wrapped around her wrist and bedpost pulled taut.

Her frightened gaze stayed fixed on the door as she debated her next move. Should she untie herself? It wouldn't be difficult to do. Should she scream for help again? Where was Anna? Would the captors really harm Anna if she didn't cooperate with their plan? *What plan?*

Shannon scanned the room. The nautical theme was not unusual for hotel décor in Door County. Her eyes examined every detail as she slowly moved her head from left to right. Her gaze landed on the sliding glass doors leading to the balcony. Could she possibly shimmy down three floors and escape? But what would happen to Anna if she tried?

Her eyes drifted from the doors to a garment bag lying over the back of one of the small leather chairs by the corner fireplace. She didn't remember seeing that before. Had they passed by it when they checked out the balcony earlier, or did someone place it there later? Shannon's eyes followed the length of the garment bag downward. A shoebox rested on the floor beneath it.

She decided to take a chance and untie her wrist. With the lame way her captor had secured her, he felt confident with the threat of Anna's well-being. Shannon would cooperate and make no further attempts to escape.

It took a couple of minutes for Shannon to undo the knot in the rope but she managed. She scooted off the bed and glanced at the door between the rooms of the suite. No movement. She stood silent for a moment, just listening. No sounds.

She kept her eyes and ears tuned to the disturbing quiet as she stepped toward the garment bag. Grasping the top of the garment bag, she lifted it up as she pulled on the zipper and revealed an elegant, vintage, off-white wedding dress. Made of silk crepe, it had short cap sleeves and a high scoop neck line open to the front of the quilted triangle waistband. A plain dress, perhaps from the forties, like her grandmother would have worn. She set the garment bag down and pulled the lid from the shoebox to find a pair of strappy, high-heeled sandals. She couldn't picture her grandmother wearing something like that with such a dress.

Shannon put the cover back on the box. What was this all about?

She stepped toward the sliding glass doors and reached to slide the vertical blinds over. She'd barely touched them, enough to catch a glimpse of daylight breaking, when the same high-pitched male voice from before echoed throughout the room. "Step away from the door."

Shannon retreated so quickly she nearly tripped, catching herself on the corner of the fireplace. Her nervous gaze searched the room for the camera and speaker. There it was, plain as day, mounted near the ceiling above the desk. How did she not see that before?

As she moved across the room, the device moved with her. She ran her hands over her shivering arms to suppress the rising goose bumps.

In an attempt to hide her fear from her captors, she dropped her arms to her sides and fixed her gaze on the camera. Absently, she placed her hand over her growling stomach in an attempt to ignore her hunger pains. How long ago had she last eaten anything? She and Anna had lunch before they traveled north to search for the second cache. She grew lightheaded at the thought of the finger they'd found. Placing the palm of her hand on the desk, she steadied herself.

"Would you like something to eat?"

Shannon shifted her eyes back to the camera. "No," she blurted firmly before her jaw clamped shut. She'd die before she'd accept anything from him, whoever he was.

"Are you sure? I can order something for you, whatever you want."

Shannon unclenched her jaw. "What I want is to be released with my friend Anna."

"That I can't do. Not until our business is resolved."

"What business?"

"Isn't it obvious?"

Shannon just stared at the camera. What in the world was he talking about?

A few beats passed. "You'll look lovely in that dress today."

Shannon's head spun in the direction of the garment bag. "The wedding dress?"

"Yes, my dear."

* * * *

Spinelli stood on the boardwalk and stared out over the frigid waters of Sturgeon Bay. The early-morning northwest wind coming off the bay was raw and stung his cheeks. How could she do this to him? Not even have the common courtesy to tell him in person that she was about to marry someone else?

To be so thoughtless and uncaring was not typical of her character. Just over twenty-four hours ago, she lay in his bed with her warm limbs entwined among his. The scent of her sex flooded his bedroom, satisfying his sense of smell beyond any level he'd ever encountered before; more than he'd ever thought conceivable. He lay with her in a completely satisfied state, both sexually and emotionally. The emotion always amazed him. Until Shannon, he'd never known such fulfillment. Only yesterday, he considered finally proposing to her--this weekend, on her birthday. He felt like such a fool.

His body quivered. How could she do this, give herself to him so fully and then turn it off so quickly to marry someone else? He shook his head. None of this made any sense. He was a detective, for crissake. He read people for a living. There was no way he misread Shannon. It just wasn't possible. Running his hand over his face, his fingers warmed. Not even forty degrees outside, yet his head was nearly ready to combust.

For lack of something better to do with them, he stuffed his hands into the pockets of his jeans as his gaze stayed glued to the dark swirling waters of the bay. He stood still, alone on the promenade, pondering his life. How had everything gone to shit so fast?

Vehicle tires hummed as they crossed the grate of the old steel bridge to his left. People were coming to life on this crappy Saturday morning. And little by little, light brightened the dingy cloud-covered sky. Not quite sure what to do with himself at this very moment, he spun on his heel and headed back toward the lobby of the hotel.

Spinelli pushed his way through the door to find Walker and Marsh still in the lobby. They stood off to the side of the room analyzing the document the waitress had delivered minutes earlier. He watched and listened unnoticed.

Marsh held the paper in his gloved hand and pulled it closer to his eyes. "It looks real."

Walker nodded. "Yeah, but there's just no way. I'm not buying it. Something's up. This is not the way she behaves. And with the call Spinelli got from her yesterday ..."

"So you think this is a fake?" Marsh summed.

"For comparison purposes, I wish we had another signature of

Shannon's," Walker said as he pointed at the document, careful not to actually touch it. "And notice how her signature extends outside the box."

"So?"

"It seems odd to me that someone as particular as Shannon would let her signature extend outside the area she'd been given to sign her name. The 'S' from her first name actually crosses over the left line of the signature box and the top line. And the 'O' from her last name extends way beyond the top line of the box. I would picture her as the type of person who would neatly tuck her signature into the box."

Spinelli rushed forward and poked his head between Walker and Marsh's. Walker was right. And deep down, he knew Shannon would never do such a thing. Nobody could fake the love they shared. He wanted to kick himself. How had he not noticed the signature issue when he looked at the marriage license earlier?

Spinelli's gaze drifted toward the other signature on the license. Who in the hell was this Davin O'Brien?

Spinelli hadn't wanted to worry any of Shannon's family until he knew more details, but perhaps it was time to call her Uncle Bernie in Milwaukee. Shannon and Bernie were close. Maybe he could help.

Bernie answered his cellphone so quickly Spinelli swore he had been waiting for him to call.

"Spinelli."

"Yeah, hi Bernie. Sorry, I know it's early but do you by chance know where Shannon is?"

Spinelli tried to wait out the agonizing, uncomfortable silence. He could hear Bernie breathing, so he knew he hadn't been cut off. "Bernie?"

"No. I don't. I've been trying to reach her myself but she's not answering her cell."

"She's not answering my calls either."

"Last I knew, she was going to Door County with Anna for some geocaching thing."

"Yeah, we're in Door County now looking for her."

"We're? What? In Door County?" Bernie sputtered.

"Me, Walker and Marsh are in Sturgeon Bay looking for Shannon. I received a strange call from her yesterday about 3:30. We got cut off and I haven't been able to reach her since."

Something clunked. Did Bernie drop his cellphone?

The sound of wood scraping against wood resonated into Spinelli's ear canal; shattering glass followed. "What have you done to her, you sawed off little runt?" Bernie growled.

"Nothing. I didn't do anything," exclaimed a high-pitched adult male voice.

"Bernie ... Bernie," Spinelli yelled into his phone. It was no use. The man had obviously dropped his phone.

"What's going on?" Walker asked.

Spinelli shrugged and shook his head, his phone still pressed to his ear. The sound of shuffling feet echoed through the line, followed by a thud.

"Where is she, you little prick?" Bernie's voice sounded even angrier than a moment ago.

"I don't know. I haven't seen her ... really. Just put me down and we'll talk about this," the unfamiliar voice pleaded.

What in the hell? "Put me down," Spinelli repeated. Did Bernie just pick up some guy? Christ, he's sixty-some years old. Who is this guy? And why would he have done something to Shannon.

It sounded like a sack of potatoes had dropped to the floor.

"Ouch, seriously? Was that necessary?"

"Shut up," Bernie snapped.

Bernie's labored breathing penetrated Spinelli's ear.

"Bernie, what's going on? Who's with you?"

"Nobody. Just an old family friend." Before Spinelli could question Bernie further, Bernie began his own line of questioning. "Tell me about this strange call from Shannon. What did she say?"

Spinelli debated his response. Should he let Bernie in on the details? At this point, they needed all the help they could get.

Spinelli expelled a breath. "She called me from one of the cache locations. She was pretty worked up. She told me she and Anna found a finger in the cache box."

"A real finger?" Bernie asked. His tone didn't seem all that surprised.

"Sounds that way."

"I see. By chance, Nick, was there a gold Claddagh ring on that finger?"

Did he really just ask me if a severed finger had a ring on it? How would he know? "Yes."

Something clunked, feet shuffled. "You little son of a bitch! I'll wring your scrawny neck. Where is she?"

"I don't know. I haven't seen her yet!"

"Ouch. You just bit me. Men don't bite. What are you, some sort of animal?"

"Let me go!"

Spinelli pulled his cell from his ear and stared at the screen. "Dammit!"

"What's happening?" Walker asked.

"I'm not sure, but I don't like it." Spinelli put the phone on speaker so they could all hear the fight on Bernie's end. "He knew about the ring on the severed finger."

"How on earth did he know that?" Marsh asked.

"That's what I'd like to find out. And evidently the person with Bernie knows Shannon and may know something about the finger."

Moments later, Bernie huffed into the phone.

"What's happening? Who are you with? And how did you know about the ring?"

After sucking in a couple more quick breaths, Bernie cleared his throat. "I'm guessing the finger belongs to my dad, Shannon's grandfather."

"I thought your dad was deceased?"

"He is. He died in 1969."

"Let me get this right. You're telling me your dead father's finger showed up in a cache box in Door County, over forty years after your father died."

"It appears so."

Chapter Four

Shannon pounded her fists against the door, demanding to be released. Maybe someone other than her captor would hear her as well.

"You'll shut up if you know what's good for your friend Anna."

Shannon silenced and halted her numbing fists. Her body tensed as an agony of rage jolted through her. She didn't like hearing this stranger say Anna's name. She drew in a long deep breath in an attempt to provide herself with the needed time to regain her sensibility. Anna's safety was priority.

Shannon pressed her forehead against the door, wondering what to do next. "What is this all about? Why are you doing this to me?" she asked in barely more than a whisper.

The door clicked. Shannon jumped back and pressed her back to the wall on the opposite side of the room. A tall, thin, older gentleman stepped through the doorway. His dark blue eyes immediately fixed on her.

Shannon studied him, wondering if she could out-maneuver him. She sighed. It didn't matter because they had Anna.

The man shut the door behind him but kept his distance. "You look scared," he said, his stone-cold eyes unwavering.

Shannon froze in place. Of course she was scared. She'd been kidnapped, held captive and separated from Anna.

"As long as you do as you're told, everything will be okay for both you and your friend."

A quick glance at the wedding dress on the back of the chair alerted her to the fact she would be married soon, but to whom and why? The man before her had to be at least as old as her father.

He must have read her mind. "Don't worry dearie, it's not me you'll be marrying today. You'll be marrying my son, making good on a promise made by your grandfather some years ago."

"Excuse me?"

"You are all that stands between me and my inheritance, which is contingent upon you marrying my eldest son."

Shannon vaguely recalled her Uncle Bernie and mother discussing from time to time a crazy story about some madman her mother was promised to marry in the old country. Evidently, the pasty, grey-haired man standing before her was the madman.

"I can see the wheels spinning in your pretty little head. It appears your family hasn't informed you of your obligation." He paused and then huffed, "but I'm not surprised. They've avoided their duty for nearly two generations, but it stops here and now. Today, you will marry my son and all debts will be paid in full. I will inherit the money due me and someday the wealth will be passed onto Davin, making you a very wealthy woman. Very wealthy," he repeated coolly. "It would be nice if you'd take on this task voluntarily, but we're prepared to make it happen either way. The choice is yours, understood?"

Shannon understood all right. They'd hurt Anna if she disagreed. Her knees went weak and she'd have fallen if she hadn't been leaning against the wall. She considered her options but found none. For Anna's sake, she'd go through with this plan and figure out how to undo everything later. Her heart nearly dropped to her feet. *So much for saying 'I do' only once.* Sweat beaded on her brow at the idea of marrying someone she didn't know, let alone love. Her breath hitched as terror snapped through her at the possibility of consummating this farce of a marriage.

Her gaze refocused on the old man before her. She needed to suck it up and drum up some courage to get herself and Anna through this disastrous event. After willing away the tears burning in the back of her eyes, she squared her shoulders. She would be darned if she'd let him see her sweat or cry.

"When will this marriage take place and when will I see Anna again?" Shannon asked, hoping to gauge how much time she had to figure a way out of this mess. With any luck, she might find a way to delay everything and give Spinelli more time to locate her. Surely, after the frantic phone call about the finger in the cached box, he'd be looking for her. *Why does this crazy crap keep happening to me?* It's like she was being punished for something. But what did the finger have to do with anything? "Wait, the ring," Shannon whispered.

"Yes, the ring."

Shannon lifted her eyes to meet the old man's again. She couldn't help but notice the evil grin on his face as well. The kind of grin bullies wore during recess on the playground. She worked to firm up her voice. "What's the deal with the ring?"

His atrocious grin grew wider. "Sent as a reminder to your Uncle Bernie as to what happens when deals are broken."

"So then why didn't you put the ring where he'd find it, rather than me?"

"Oh, but that wouldn't have delivered the kind of impact I hoped to achieve."

He stepped forward slowly, edging closer toward her. His ice-cold gaze pinned her in place. The sheer intensity of his stare alerted her to the fact that he was beyond 'bully' status; he was simply mad. Reaching up, he skimmed the back of his long, ice-cold fingers over her cheek. His hand was soft like a woman's. His stale breath brushed over her face. Shannon pressed the back of her head tighter to the wall. "But he doesn't even know that …"

The old man snugly gripped her chin between his thumb and forefinger, glanced at his watch, and then shifted his gaze back to hers. "Oh trust me, dearie, by now he knows. And I'm guessing he's rethinking his past choices."

What in the world is this idiotic old man talking about? What choices? Stay strong. Shannon jerked her head to the side to break free from his hold, hoping her abrupt movement would send him a message.

* * * *

Spinelli paced the floor waiting for Bernie to phone back. Bernie had disconnected the call abruptly after their initial conversation in regard to the finger and ring. Spinelli didn't get to ask any of the numerous follow-up questions that flooded his mind. However, he found some comfort in Bernie's assurance to call with more details the second they got on the road. *They--who exactly were 'they?'*

Spinelli placed his cell phone on the small round table in his hotel room. He, Walker and Marsh stared at it, as if their impatience would cause Bernie to call back quicker. Spinelli was dying to hear an explanation about the forty-year-old dismembered finger. His patience shot, he slammed his fist against the table and jolted the phone into ringing mode. Okay, coincidental, but it didn't matter. The release of anger made him feel better for a split second.

Walker tapped the speaker button on the phone so they could all hear Bernie.

Spinelli leaned toward the phone. "What in the hell is going on?"

"We just left Milwaukee and are headed North on I43. We should be there in less than three hours."

"That's fine, but what's this all about? And who's with you?"

After a brief hesitation, Bernie spoke, "It's going to sound ridiculous, but this whole thing is a result of the marriage of my grandparents, Shannon's great-grandparents."

"Excuse me?"

"The crazy bastard is trying to make good on a deal struck between my father and his."

"I thought you said it was your grandparents, now it's your father? And who's the crazy bastard you're talking about? What's the deal?" Spinelli asked, unable to keep the agitation from his tone.

"That's what I'm getting to. You need to give me a minute to get this in order," Bernie replied with unmistakable frustration.

Spinelli glanced from the phone to Walker. Walker's look was enough for Spinelli to know he needed to zip it up and give Bernie a chance to explain.

"I'm sorry, Bernie. I'm just a bit confused as to what in the hell is going on here."

"Yeah, I know, I get it. Unfortunately, Nick, I'm afraid it will get worse before it gets better. It's a long convoluted story, and I'll do my best to explain it all from the beginning."

The millisecond of a pause gave Spinelli enough time to catch another silencing glance from Walker; one for good-measure.

43

"We're ready to listen, Bernie," Walker replied to verbally reconfirm the fact that Spinelli would not interrupt.

"Okay. It all started in the mid 1920's. My grandfather, Graham Mathison, was a student at Oxford when he met my grandmother. After a short courtship, they were married in a private ceremony. When she returned to Ireland with an English husband, the shit hit the fan. She was an only child and had been promised by her father to marry Tomas O'Brien. Both my grandmother's parents and Tomas' parents were wealthy landowners and they viewed this union as a way to increase their wealth and stature. Hence, the Mathison and O'Brien feud began."

Marsh pulled a frown. "An arranged marriage started all this trouble? You've got to be kidding me."

Walker cocked his head to the side and fixed his silencing glare on Marsh before Spinelli had the chance.

"No, I'm not kidding, that's what started the whole ugly feud. Things were different back then. Anyhow, Tomas eventually married and had two sons, Emmet and one that died in an accident when he was just a teenager. My grandparents had three boys: my father Winston and my two uncles. Seeing as both unions only yielded boys, they had no options of marriage to join the wealth as promised by the earlier generation. Though Tomas married someone else, he still felt he'd been wronged and demanded restitution. Graham refused so Tomas did anything he could to make my grandfather's life a living hell."

Spinelli massaged his throbbing temples as he waited out Bernie's audible breaths.

He was just about to urge Bernie to continue when he started up again. "In the meantime, my father and Emmet, the eldest son in each family, became schoolmates and best buddies. Despite the feud and their father's demands, neither wanted to disband the friendship. They came up with a plan to satisfy their fathers and get them off their backs. Emmet and Winston agreed that their children would make good on the deal. They sealed the deal with the exchange of gold Claddagh friendship rings. Emmet had two sons, one who died at a young age and Riordan. As you are aware, my father had Mary, Shannon's mother and me. According to the agreement Mary and Riordan should have married to make good on the promise and end the family feud."

Bernie paused. Was he done with the story or realigning his thoughts? Spinelli leaned closer to the phone. "What happened? I mean, obviously Mary and Riordan never married, right?"

Bernie cleared his throat. "As you are probably aware, Northern Ireland was really not the place to be in the late 60's. At my father's request, Mary and I moved to England but my mother refused to leave her homestead. I was already out of high school and Mary needed to finish up her last year. We stayed with relatives until she graduated. With the political climate in such turmoil, it wasn't safe to go back to Ireland. We stayed in England for a bit longer and Mary started college. In the meantime, Riordan really flipped out. He wasn't right in the head to begin with, but with all the protesting between the Catholics and Protestants, he really wigged out. His father did as well."

The rising pitch of Bernie's voice informed Spinelli that Bernie was reliving the events as he told the story.

"Take a breather, Bernie. Continue when you're ready," Walker instructed.

A few more beats of silence passed before Bernie pressed forward. "My father reached the point where he wanted nothing to do with either of them. They accused my father of sending Mary away to avoid a marriage to Riordan. I believe, to this day, Emmet may have been partially right. I could see how my father did not want his only daughter to marry an extremist such as Riordan. And I'm sure Mary's pleas to get out of the deal didn't help matters either. While Mary and I were in England, our father grew ill and passed away. Our mother insisted we not return for the funeral and eventually, she abandoned her homestead and moved to England as well."

"What about the finger?" Spinelli couldn't help but ask.

Bernie's sigh echoed through the phone. "His finger was removed sometime during the wake period. My mother always believed that Emmet or Riordan cut it off as a means to prevent my father's soul from resting in peace. Though she could never prove how they did it without anyone noticing. I don't think a day went by that she didn't regret leaving that friendship ring on his finger. But he always wore it, even after the falling out. My mother believed he continued to wear it because, deep down, my father hoped to make amends with Emmet."

"So you're saying that during the wake, when people milled about and paid their respects, no one noticed someone slice off his finger?" Spinelli asked.

"Well, you have to remember, wake periods were a little different back then. My father died at home. His body never left the house until we turned it over to the church the evening before the burial. The wake period lasts from the time of death to the time the body is conveyed to the church. The body is never left unattended. Someone, usually a woman, always sat with the body. Evidently, there weren't a lot of people around at the time his finger was cut off, probably just one person."

"So the finger was removed from the body while it was attended?" Spinelli's questioning came faster with each exchange.

"Yep, sliced right out from among the rosary beads woven within his fingers."

"Who sat with the body during the time this happened?"

"A neighbor lady. My mother found her hunched over in her chair, sleeping. She had to shake her to wake her. As the story goes, she didn't wake easy but when she did, she was disoriented and mumbled something about a crackling sound, blinding light and dense fog. The next thing she remembered was my mother waking her. She complained of a burning sensation in her nostrils and a strong metallic taste on her tongue. She wasn't sure what exactly happened, but she wasted no time getting the hell out of there once they'd discovered the missing finger. She mumbled something about evil spirits as she ran out of the house."

"What in the hell?"

"What?" Bernie asked.

Spinelli shot a glance at Walker who also wore a baffled look. "Early this morning I heard a crackling noise, followed by an acidic scent that made my nose prickle. Walker experienced something similar. I just find that kind of bizarre."

"Hmm," Bernie responded. A few beats of silence passed. "If you know anything about this you'd better speak up."

The person with Bernie cleared his throat. "From the sound of it, I guess it's possible my dad is here making good on the deal."

"Yeah, it sounds that way," Bernie replied.

The brief conversation on the other end of the line reminded Spinelli of the other person in the car with Bernie. "Who's with you?"

"Davin O'Brien."

Spinelli's mouth fell open but no words escaped.

Marsh glanced at the copy of the marriage license and then looked at Spinelli. "That's the name on the license all right. I guess they're getting what they want. Shannon's bridegroom is en route."

"Marriage license?" Bernie repeated.

"Yeah, someone dropped off a copy of a marriage license which indicates that Shannon is to be married to a Davin O'Brien. Today," Walker replied.

Bernie growled. Spinelli could only imagine the 'look to kill' he now gave Davin.

"I don't know anything about the marriage license. I just came to see you, as the responsible generation, to discuss the deal." Davin spat back.

"What's the rush, why now?" Bernie asked.

"Because my grandfather is dying. He only has a few days left, tops. He blames my dad for losing his best friend, your father, all those years ago. He claims if it hadn't been for my dad's extremist ways, your sister wouldn't have been afraid to marry him and make good on the deal."

"I doubt Emmet really gave a shit about losing his best friend. He's pissed about the damned land he wanted."

Davin didn't deny Bernie's accusation. "Anyhow, my grandfather has threatened to leave everything to the university upon his death, rather than my father, unless my father can make good on the deal. You know the situation, Bernie. My dad hasn't worked a day in his life. He's lived off grandfather's wealth all this time. He'll have nothing."

"Nothing unless Shannon marries you. You two are all that is left at present to seal the deal."

"Yep."

"And you'll have nothing unless the marriage takes place. So there's no reason for me to believe that you aren't part of this little plan," Bernie accused. His tone grew stiffer with each passing syllable. "So you know where she is, where your father is keeping her."

"No, I don't know where she is. I came here by myself to try to reason with you," Davin responded.

Spinelli's patience was about shot. "So you're telling us that your family planned to come here and abduct Shannon, force her to marry you in order to secure an inheritance and some property, as a result of a deal originally made over one hundred years ago? You do realize that unless you hide her from the world for the rest of her life, this isn't going to work, right? I will find her, and you and your family will pay dearly!" Spinelli's fists shook the table, nearly bouncing the cell phone over the edge.

"I told you, I didn't have anything to do with her disappearance! I thought I could reason with her and Bernie. I hoped the wealth she acquired would be enough incentive for her to help us out. According to the instructions my grandfather gave his lawyer, my family would get sizeable annual payments from my grandfather's estate, commencing on the day of our wedding. The remainder of the estate would be paid out on our fifth anniversary. I just figured she and I could part ways at that time, both in a decent financial situation and put this whole thing behind us."

"Have you ever met Shannon?" Spinelli asked.

"No."

"Well if you had, you'd know she'd never go for something like this, marrying someone she didn't love for a few dollars or over a few acres of land."

"It's not just a few dollars and a few acres of land, Mr. Spinelli. We're talking tens of millions of dollars and a couple thousand acres of land," Davin replied in a tone much calmer, and more confident, than he'd used just minutes ago. "Let me ask you this, are you sure you want to stand in the way of a secure monetary future?"

Spinelli swallowed hard as he thought about Davin's words. Financially, Shannon would be set for life with this union. Did he want to stand in the way of her security? Once she found out about the wealth, would he even be able to stand in the way? He sighed. In his experience, money always changed everything. Even though he knew Shannon was not a material person, his fists tightened as his haunting insecurity engulfed him. He worked to tamp down his rising anxiety and refocused. "With that much money, what does Emmet need the land for?"

"It's the principle of the matter for him," Davin replied without hesitation.

"Bernie, you and Shannon's mom own a couple of thousand acres in Ireland?"

"Yeah, we did at one time, but we sold off three hundred acres several years back."

"Do you ever go there?"

"No, neither Mary nor I have been back since the day our parents shipped us off to England. We really wanted nothing to do with it. The memories of the place toward the end, and our father's untimely death there, just turned us off. But when Mary and I needed money for our kids' college tuition, we sold some of the land."

"I know it probably equates to a lot of cash but do I dare ask, then, why you just don't give it to Emmet and end all this turmoil? Or sell it to him for a reasonable price?"

Bernie sighed. "I guess it's the principle of the matter. They cut off my dad's finger."

Spinelli squeezed his eyes shut. *Seriously. Stubbornness, passed down from one generation to another.*

"Davin, call your father and tell him he can have the land if he just returns Shannon and Anna safely," Bernie demanded.

"That won't work."

"Why not?" Bernie asked in frustration.

Moments of silence filled the air.

"Davin, what's the problem? Why won't your father agree to that arrangement?" Walker asked.

"There's one more condition in my grandfather's demands."

"And that is?" Walker pushed forward.

Davin expelled a lengthy breath. "She and I are to produce a male heir in the five year time frame. If we don't, the remainder of the estate goes to the university."

Spinelli's heart leaped into his throat. Now they expected her to have children with a man she didn't even know, in order to secure their inheritance. Was this just some sort of sick joke? They couldn't possibly be serious, in this day and age.

Chapter Five

Shannon sat on the edge of the bed and stared at the wedding dress lying over the back of the chair. Like many other females, she'd dreamed of her wedding day since she was a little girl. She pictured herself in an elegant white dress with a long flowing train; her arm hooked with her father's, as he walked her down the aisle lined with rose petals. They nodded at the smiling faces of family and friends as she floated toward her handsome bridegroom. Until recently, she'd never been able to see the groom's face. Now Spinelli waited for her at the altar, his smoldering charcoal gaze fixed on her, as if she were the only person in the room. What he did for a tuxedo should be illegal. The thoughts reeling through her mind of 'wedding' daydreams as she walked toward him sent her cheeks to a point just below flaming. Who was she kidding? More than her cheeks flamed at the sight of him and the thought of his touch.

As a young lady, she'd pictured herself with someone totally different from Spinelli, someone quieter and reserved like her dad. Yet she couldn't help but fall in love with Spinelli and his 'take the bull by the horns' demeanor. At least, that's how he appeared on the surface. But she knew better. His thoughtful, caring and sensitive nature had shown through on more than one occasion in the few short months since she first met him.

His relationship with the Washington children had stolen her heart. While on assignment together, they had removed the kids from their house and brought them to their new foster home. The removal incident hadn't gone well, but the events that followed were absolutely touching. Spinelli took those kids under his wing, and to this day, went out of his way to make them feel loved; something he'd never known as a child.

Raised sporadically by a young drug-addicted mother, he had been passed around from foster home to foster home. Shannon knew Spinelli would probably never say the words, but his actions let the kids know he loved and cared for them.

Shannon lay back on the bed, fully intending to allow tender thoughts of Spinelli to distract her from the upcoming events of the day. She placed her right hand over her aching chest; her heart thudded against her palm. The mere thought of him lying next to her increased the already rapid rhythm.

She closed her eyes in an attempt to fully indulge herself. The warmth of Spinelli's love surrounded and comforted her. His masculine woodsy scent flooded her nostrils. Her extremities tingled at the mere thought of him touching her as he'd done earlier the previous day. Their lovemaking had continued from the night before, into the wee morning hours.

Spinelli, a pleasingly slow lover, almost tormented her at times as his deliberate actions often had her begging him for completion. Shannon could never quite figure which she liked more: his unbridling talent in edging her toward orgasm, his uncanny ability to hold her on the rim of ecstasy and milk it for all it's worth, or his aptitude for knowing just the right time to push her over the edge. Perhaps it was the aftermath of their lovemaking and simply lying in his arms. On the other hand, there were occasions when Spinelli was a hurried, greedy lover. Shannon equally enjoyed these times, when his primal need was so strong he couldn't seem to think clearly. She relished her power over him during those times when the tables were turned. She knew just how to push his buttons to drive him to the verge of begging.

Prior to Spinelli, Shannon hadn't had much experience with lovers, and she'd realized that from the first moment his lips touched hers he'd be her last lover. Who was she kidding? She knew from his very first dazed gaze she was a goner. She remembered that first look from him as clearly as if it had happened yesterday. He had reported for duty in her department, and rung his bell pretty good when he tripped and took a header into the receptionist's desk. As Shannon helped to steady him, he worked to gather himself as he stared at her like a deer in the headlights. With each passing beat, the haziness in his gaze cleared and transformed into one of the most intense looks she'd ever encountered. His dark charcoal eyes were nearly black by the time she released his arm, and she was sure he'd seen directly into her soul. Of course, it was possible his strange transitioning gaze may have had something to do with the fall he took. She preferred to believe it was a direct result of his realization that he was staring into the eyes of his soul mate.

Shannon's awful situation didn't prevent the corners of her mouth from lifting upward as she thought about her and Spinelli's zany little meet-cute. He'd been temporarily re-assigned from the homicide division to help her in social services with child placement for the holiday season. The holiday season seemed to be an extremely tough time of year for her clientele; so at times law enforcement accompanied the social workers to their home visits in the less than desirable areas in the city. During this particular past holiday season, it happened that most of her home visits took place in some pretty tough areas of town. In fact, neighborhoods Spinelli was all too familiar with, both professionally and personally.

Though Shannon prided herself on being a strong, independent woman, she couldn't help resist Spinelli's alpha-male tendencies. She'd thanked God on more than one occasion for his over-protective nature. And from the way things were turning out today, she hoped for the opportunity to offer another thank you.

A tear slid down her cheek. Would she ever see him again? Feel his strong arms wrapped around her and bathe in the comfort of his love? And who will take care of him if she doesn't get out of this mess? He didn't think he needed taking care of, but she knew better; and in her heart, she knew she was the one chosen for him.

* * * *

Spinelli grabbed the Door County visitor guide from the desk in his hotel room and flipped to the index. He skimmed his finger over the rows of verbiage until he located the words 'Places of Worship.' "Page 156," he whispered before he flipped to that page. An exaggerated sigh escaped him. "You've got to be kidding me."

"What?" Walker asked as he craned his head over Spinelli's shoulder.

"There's got to be over fifty churches in this county." Spinelli glanced at the clock. Nearly 7:30. How would they be able to cover that many places for any scheduled weddings?

"Well, we probably only need to cover the Catholic churches," Walker piped in. "How many of those?"

"You're right. From the way it sounds, Emmet wouldn't stand for anything other than a good ole Catholic union." Spinelli glanced back at the directory. "It looks like there are about ten."

"We can plot them out and start with the ones right here in Sturgeon Bay," Walker offered.

Spinelli's chest constricted. "What if it's done already?"

"It can't be."

Spinelli just stared at Walker.

"They don't have the groom and won't until 10:00 or so. And in the event Davin's truly not in cahoots with the real abductors, we need to figure out how they intend on getting their hands on him. That said, I can only assume they've lined something up here in town as to save time," Walker said as he grabbed Spinelli's laptop, cracked it open and started plotting all the Door County Catholic churches on the map.

Spinelli swallowed the lump in his throat. "What if Davin's just a decoy and Riordan marries Shannon? Maybe Emmet doesn't really care who makes good on the deal as long as it's done."

Walker stopped clicking keys and scratched his chin. "Well for one thing, they'd need a marriage license with both Riordan and Shannon's name on it."

"Yeah, true, but how hard is that to get? They already bought one with Shannon and Davin's names."

Marsh bounded into the room with a satisfied grin on his face, his little spiraled notebook in one hand and a few 8 ½ by 11 sheets in his other hand.

"What do you have?" Spinelli asked.

Marsh's smile grew. "Oh, just a detailed description of the man who delivered the envelope with the bogus marriage license to the waitress, and a couple still-shots of him from the resort's surveillance system. The photos aren't great, but between them and the description the waitress gave we have a little something to go on."

"Just to verify, the waitress had never seen him before?" Spinelli asked.

"Nope, nor did any of the other staff who worked this morning. I asked them all."

The first photo caught a shot of the deliveryman talking to the waitress at the restaurant's checkout station. The man, dressed in jeans and a bright green hoodie with the hood up, wore a jacket zipped to the top. The photo was blurry. Spinelli assumed the poor quality was a result of exporting a still-shot taken from a video recording. But even through the fuzziness and narrow opening of the hoodie, he could see the man's dark goatee, high cheekbones and narrow chin.

According to Marsh, the waitress figured the man to be in his late twenties or early thirties with dark brown eyes.

The second photo showed the man exiting the hotel through the front lobby doors. Judging from the clearance between the top of the man's head and the doorframe, he looked to be slightly less than six feet tall and of medium build.

Spinelli sighed. "Great, we're looking for a guy of medium height and build, with dark hair and brown eyes. Yeah, he should be easy to find," Spinelli growled. Seriously, why did Marsh look so happy about this? Probably 2,000 men in this small town fit that average-Joe description.

"Take another look at the photo of the man exiting the building," Marsh suggested, his smile now stretching from ear to ear.

Spinelli pulled the photo closer to his eyes. Walker leaned in to get a better look before he lifted his finger and pointed at a blurry picture and patch of words, silk-screened on the hoodie across the man's back. "What is that a picture of? And what does it say?"

Spinelli squinted. "It looks like a four leaf clover, but I can't make out the words. I wonder if we can blow it up."

Marsh cleared his throat. "I knew you'd ask that," he replied as he handed Spinelli a third printout with a larger, clearer version of the picture.

Spinelli sucked in a slow breath and silently counted to ten. Why hadn't Marsh just shown this picture to them in the first place? Why did he always have to play these little games? Ten seconds of Spinelli's life he couldn't have back. Ten seconds of time wasted in search of Shannon and Anna. Did Marsh not realize how important ten seconds could be? Spinelli refocused, he couldn't chance losing any more time. He'd deal with Marsh later.

With the larger picture, there was no need to squint, the white four-leaf clover nearly leaped off the page along with the words 'McGrath Clan.'

Walker sat in front of the laptop and googled 'McGrath,' narrowing his search to Door County. Several names flashed across the screen and their locations peppered the entire county, including Washington Island. Hoping this McGrath still had a landline, they'd start calling all the numbers immediately in hopes to reach anyone who could identify the man in the picture. Once they locate the deliveryman, perhaps he could shed some light on who asked him to deliver the package and why, where, when and how he'd been contacted for the job.

Walker stood with the laptop in his hands. "I'll run downstairs and see if I can use the hotel's printer to make some copies of the plotted maps, contact information and the McGrath contact list. We can split them up and start searching."

Spinelli grabbed his coat and followed, Marsh in tow.

Marsh went to get the car, Walker printed off the documents in the hotel's business center and Spinelli talked with some of the hotel staff. Walker returned a moment later with the laptop in one hand and a fist full of papers in the other.

"Okay, so we only have two churches to check out right here in the city. We'll go to the one on the east side of town first," Walker said as he climbed into the backseat.

Spinelli slipped into the passenger seat.

Marsh exited the parking lot and Spinelli motioned for him to turn left at the stop sign. He drove up another four blocks before Spinelli told him to hang a left. Walker clicked on the keyboard in the backseat until Marsh pulled up to the curb and parked in front of the church.

Walker leaned between the seats. "There aren't any weddings listed in March on the church's website. But who knows, maybe they don't list them there or maybe this was scheduled so late they didn't list it on the calendar."

Spinelli stared out his window at the multiple rows of stone steps leading to the front doors of the church. The weathered stone church with twin towering steeples looked exactly like what he envisioned Shannon would marry in someday. In fact, it looked a great deal like the church she belonged to in Milwaukee, only smaller.

At present, the building looked quiet but it was early.

Walker leaned between the front seats again, his phone still pressed to his ear. "I got the church's answering machine. According to their automated attendant, they don't have regular office hours on Saturdays, and it doesn't mention an alternative number to call."

Marsh flipped the car in reverse and slowly backed up a couple of car lengths.

"What are you doing?" Spinelli asked.

Once he reached the corner of the street, Marsh put the car in park again and pointed out Spinelli's window. "The church has a sign over there. Maybe it lists the daily events. Can you read it?"

"Not from here," Spinelli responded as he flung his door open. With a few long strides, he found himself combing over the church's regular mass schedule through the glass of the church's display sign.

He raked his fingers through his hair as he eyed the words on the sign again. Nothing. A frustrated laugh escaped him. What did he expect? That the sign would actually read, "Here Spinelli, you're on the right track, this is the church where Shannon will be forced to marry some stranger today in order to secure his inheritance."

Shifting his gaze back to the church, he glanced up at the twin towers. They looked like silent guardians meant to protect those who enter their place of worship. An aura of peace seemed to surround them. Spinelli found himself secretly asking them to watch over Shannon if she entered here today.

Spinelli tore his gaze from the steeples and fixed it on the stained glass windows lining the side of the church. The dingy, gloomy day darkened the normally bright stain-glass windows. Was it some sort of sign? Spinelli squeezed his eyes shut and took a moment to tamp down the irrational thoughts that invaded his mind. They would be of no use in finding Shannon. Spinelli stuffed his cold fingers into his pockets and spun on his heel. He hadn't taken two steps before a spurt of warm air brushed over him from behind. He spun around to find a bright ray of sun pierce through the overcast sky, shining directly on him. His gaze glued to the beam. The narrow opening in the clouds shifted, causing the beam to move slowly until it reached the side of the church. The ray landed on a set of two small rectangle stained glass windows. They were shorter, slimmer and shaped differently than the rest of the tall arched windows lining the length of the church wall. Spinelli hardly noticed the single flowers located in the center of each of the two windows before the bright ray disappeared as if someone shut it off with the flip of a switch. The blue hue spawned by the overcast sky darkened the windows blending the colors into one gray mass. Another sign?

Spinelli shot a glance to the sky and considered praying. What could it hurt?

Though Walker's phone call to the church's office went unanswered, Spinelli couldn't resist the urge to test the side door of the church. It was locked tight. He stepped around the corner and scooted up the stone steps leading to the church's grand entrance, taking two at a time. Those doors were locked as well.

As Spinelli slid into the car, he couldn't help but catch the strange looks on Marsh and Walker's faces. "What?"

"That was just the weirdest thing," Marsh replied.

"What do you mean? What was weird?"

"Just as you stepped away from the sign we were joking about how the church might crumble to pieces if you actually entered it. Then it was like the freaking clouds parted and put some sort of spotlight on you. I swear on my grandmother's grave, it was like you were glowing."

Spinelli gave his hard-eyed scowl to shut Marsh up.

Walker leaned forward and pointed out the windshield. "Take a left at the corner, go around the block, and get back onto Michigan Street. Hang a right and then head over that junky old steel bridge next to the hotel. According to this map, it looks like there's a Catholic church located on the block between Maple Street and Juniper. It doesn't look that far away."

Marsh did as Walker instructed.

Spinelli huffed.

"What?" Walker asked.

"We're never going to find her this way. It's too early. Nobody will be at these churches."

"Well, I'm not sure what else you want us to do right now. We've got nothing further to go on at the moment. I'm monitoring Shannon and Anna's credit cards. There's been no activity since yesterday when they checked into the hotel. We don't have enough reasonable cause to ping their cell phones yet. And every church contact number goes unanswered as well," Walker replied.

Spinelli sank further into his seat. "I know you're doing what you can."

Marsh drove past the main downtown area. Spinelli looked up and down each cross street. The city looked deserted.

Just as Marsh pulled onto the dated bridge, the red lights flashed and the gates dropped down, stopping what little traffic moved about. A loud, low-tone grinding noise started the second the bridge-tender set the draw in motion to open. Spinelli eyed the slow-moving, thousand-foot freighter as it edged its way toward the open draw. At the rate the ship moved, Spinelli was sure he'd be fifty years old before it passed completely through and allowed the draw to close again. *Now of all times!*

The second Marsh pointed at the ship, Spinelli knew they were in trouble. He didn't dare look at Marsh and encourage him to ramble on with useless information about large cargo-moving vessels or bridges.

"It's hard to imagine a ship that size actually fits through the opening in this small drawbridge," Walker commented, causing Spinelli to cringe knowing he just gave Marsh the open ticket to share his wisdom.

"Well, lucky for us we'll see it firsthand." Marsh beamed as excitedly as a kid in a candy store did. "It's my understanding that these large ships lay over for the winter at Bay Shipbuilding, once the Soo Locks close for their annual maintenance in January. Some of the ships are as long as one thousand feet and over one hundred feet wide. I read somewhere that as many as fifteen or so dock in this port. Of course, some of them are only seven to eight hundred feet long. Oh, and just for the record, this bridge opening is 140 feet wide."

Spinelli stared out the window and wondered if jumping off the bridge into the icy waters would be less painful than listing to Marsh.

Marsh cleared his throat before he continued, "You know, I've always wanted to take a trip up to Sault Ste. Marie, Michigan, and check out the Soo Locks. It must be a fascinating sight when the ships pass through. There are two canals and four locks for vessels to negotiate the 21-foot elevation drop of the St. Mary's river connecting Lake Superior, Michigan, and Huron. You know how the Soo Locks got their name?"

Spinelli didn't dare answer honestly because 'no' would surely inspire Marsh to continue. Plunging into the icy waters was really beginning to look like the preferred option.

"As a matter of fact I do, so there's no need to go there," Walker stated flatly before he changed the subject and reiterated the directions to the next church. After what seemed like an eternity, the draw closed and Marsh drove to the church. Pulling into the small parking lot near the entranceway to the parochial school, he drove into the stall next to where a minivan had just parked. He slid down his window and waved at the woman in the van. She didn't appear afraid to talk to three strange men and rolled down her window as well. The benefits of a small town, Spinelli supposed.

Marsh cleared his throat. "Good morning. Can you tell me if there is a wedding scheduled at this church today?"

The woman's warm smile radiated with kindness. "Yes. In fact, I'm here to drop off the floral arrangements."

Spinelli's heart leaped into his throat. He feared, yet welcomed, the woman's answer to what he knew would be Marsh's next question.

"Can you tell me the names of the bride and groom?"

"Sure can. The bride is my niece, Morgan Hansen, and the groom is Ryan Baudhuin. Are you relatives of the groom?"

Marsh shook his head. "No, ma'am, we have the wrong church."

The woman cocked a brow. "What is the name of the church you're trying to find?"

"Honestly, we don't know. We forgot the invitation and someone," Marsh answered with a glare at Walker, "forgot to plug the address into his phone like he said he would. All we remember between the three of us is that it is a catholic church in Door County. You're not delivering to anymore churches today, are you?"

59

"The only other wedding we have today is the Bley wedding at the Lutheran church in Egg Harbor."

"Are you the only floral shop in town?"

"Nope, beside us there's one on 3rd Avenue and one on County S, plus the grocery stores do floral arrangements for weddings as well."

Spinelli hadn't thought to check with the floral shops for wedding schedules. Though he doubted Shannon's captors took the time or cared enough to have flowers at the wedding. Checking with the floral shops could help reduce the number of churches to contact, unless of course, the church had more than one wedding booked for the day. It's not like Shannon and Davin's wedding would take very long. Spinelli imagined there'd be no guests, no hoopla, just the 'I do's.' The mere thought of it made him nauseous.

Marsh thanked the nice lady for her time as Walker googled the location of the floral shops.

"We may as well go to the floral shop on County S first. It doesn't look like it's that far from here. Marsh hung a left on Duluth Avenue. With the help of the grimly lit sky, they could easily see the stoplights lying ahead at the highway intersection. The green light illuminated a wide radius. Crossing over the highway, Walker leaned forward and held his phone between the front seats so Spinelli could look at the screen. The purple bubble indicating the location of the shop was just ahead on the left. Spinelli pointed in that direction letting Marsh know they were nearly there.

Marsh signaled and turned in to the driveway. Spinelli shot out of the car before Marsh put it in park. Walker stayed in the car to call all the McGraths on his list in hope of finding the man who delivered the marriage license to Spinelli.

Bells clinked against the glass door as Spinelli pushed his way through. He ignored them and kept his attention focused on a woman behind the counter snipping the stems of a flower. Not just any flower, but a hot-pink lily with a white edge. *Figures. Of all the flowers, it has to be the flower of death. How could such a heavenly looking flower symbolize something so awful?* Why was he thinking about the flower's meaning? Who cared? In fact, if it hadn't been for his psycho ex-girlfriend, who went by the alias 'Lady Lily,' he wouldn't have known anything about the death flower. A month ago, that crazy woman had murdered all of Shannon's past love interests. He was next on her list, but they caught her in time. Now the stupid *death* flower haunted him again. Was this some sort of sign? Spinelli inhaled. The lily's fragrance was strong, almost overwhelming. He fought his building sneeze.

The woman set the flower down and caught Spinelli's gaze. "It's a Stargazer Lily." She smiled warmly. "They mean purity, prosperity or hope."

'Hope' was all Spinelli had to go on right now.

"I thought the lily was the flower of death," Marsh interjected.

The woman pulled a frown. "Hmm, you know, I've heard that about the Red Spider Lily but this is a beautiful Stargazer."

Spinelli nearly rolled his eyes. More useless information for Marsh to store in his encyclopedia brain and bring up at some inopportune time in the future.

The woman shifted her curious gaze between the two of them. "What can I do for you gentlemen today?"

Marsh stepped forward. "We're wondering if you are doing any weddings today."

The woman cocked a brow.

Marsh blew out an exaggerated sigh, "At the risk of sounding like idiot males, here's the deal. We drove up here from Milwaukee to attend our friend's daughter's wedding only we forgot the invitation and directions to the church. All we can remember is that it is a Catholic church in Door County."

The woman shook her head and chuckled. "We have one wedding today at the Catholic church in Maplewood."

"Maplewood," Marsh repeated.

"Yeah, it's not far from here. It's about a ten-minute drive, and the wedding isn't until 1:00. Julie's working on the arrangements in the back as we speak."

"The names?"

The woman reached under the counter, grabbed a spiral notebook and flipped it open. Running her finger down the page, she stopped midway down the page and giggled. "Oh, now I remember. It's an Irish name," she said as she looked up at Marsh.

Bile rose in Spinelli's throat as her words ran through his head again. *It's an Irish name.* The words tormented him as they cycled through his mind again.

"What's so funny?" Marsh asked.

"Both the bride and groom are Irish. I guess I just find it funny they're getting married on Saint Patrick's Day weekend. The people here take the Saint Patty's Day celebration pretty serious. You know a big parade downtown, costumes, green beer, the whole nine yards."

Spinelli hoped his ears had deceived him, seriously, both parties are Irish. What are the odds this could be someone else's wedding and not Shannon O'Hara and Davin O'Brien's? Deep down, he still hoped this was all just some crazy nightmare. His throat burned and he swallowed hard tamping down the bile. Like a whip, relief snapped through him. At least now, he knew where to find them and could stop this farce of a wedding.

"The bride's name is McGinnis and the groom's is Callahan."

Spinelli lungs emptied, another dead-end.

Chapter Six

Though Shannon's brain worked to devise an escape plan, she knew it would be of no use. She had no idea where their captor, or captors, held Anna or what their reaction would truly be if she managed to escape. The old man, Riordan, scared her. One look into his hollow, uncaring eyes, told her he'd stop at nothing to secure his inheritance. Anna's well-being weighted down Shannon's shoulders. How did she always end up in these inconceivable messes? It was the like the gods themselves had cursed her.

Glancing up, she eyed the camera mounted to the ceiling. She considered tearing it down but decided it would provide no benefit either. Her captors would just tie her up or worse. She wondered if the bathroom was wired as well. She really needed to go but didn't like the idea of being watched.

Shannon's gaze fixed on the small notepad lying on the desk with the hotel's logo, 'Harbor Resort' stamped in the upper left-hand corner. A cheap Bic pen lay next to the notebook with 'Door County Resort and Conference Center' printed along the side. She normally loved Door County. Everyone loved Door County. But she didn't love it so much today and would give anything to be as far away from this place as possible.

The notebook nearly screamed her name when she looked away. She fought the urge to journal her stress away; a technique she'd learned in college and utilized on a regular basis. In her line of work, it wasn't appropriate to share details of her experiences about her clientele so journaling had become her outlet to relieve the weight she carried on their behalf. Sometimes she wondered why she cared so much. Most times, she felt like she cared more for the children she represented than their own parents did.

Shannon closed her eyes and drew in slow deep breaths. She needed to journal. She could feel herself coming unglued. When she wrote, she entered her own private little world. But the mere thought of her captors having access to what she wrote, knowing her so intimately, made her cringe. She reached down to grab the notebook when she remembered the camera. Maybe they wouldn't even let her write. They'd probably take the notebook away.

Anxiety tightened in the pit of her stomach. She needed to get out of her captor's view. Was anywhere in this suite sacred? Perhaps the bathroom. Would they really have the audacity to watcher her in there?

She shot inside the small room and slammed the door, looking for a camera or recording device. There didn't appear to be many options to hide such devices but what did she know about such things? She was a caseworker, not a law enforcement officer. Though she hadn't used the toilet, she flushed it anyhow.

Her hand itched to journal as badly as her brain yearned for it. *Think! I need that notepad or I'll go insane.*

Shannon's gaze swept the room again and stopped on the stack of towels on the metal rack. *That's it!* Her spirits lifted as she devised a plan to get the notepad off the desk unnoticed. She grabbed a towel from the metal rack next to the shower, bolted out of the bathroom and threw the towel on the desk, covering the notepad and pen. Then she knocked on the door connecting her room to the main living area of the suite.

"What do you want?" Riordan's steel voice sounded through the closed door.

"Am I allowed to take a shower?"

"Yes, but don't dilly dally. We're leaving in an hour."

Shannon's heart thudded in her chest. *An hour.* Her spongy knees held only long enough for her to take a seat at the desk. She leaned forward, and wept into the towel she'd thrown on the surface moments ago. Her stomach tossed from both nerves and hunger. Swallowing hard, she sat upright and scooped up the towel making sure to pick up the notepad and pen within the folds of the towel, hoping Riordan wouldn't notice.

Crazed Reckoning

Once in the bathroom, Shannon pulled the notepad and pen from the towel and tossed the cloth on the counter. She sat on the toilet seat and began to journal. Her fingers, as if they had a mind of their own, gripped the pen and made cursive motions. She didn't care if it made sense, that wasn't the point. She let herself go, filling the first page in no time, then the second, then the third. As she flipped to the fourth page, she knew this would not solve her problem but the weight on her shoulders eased slightly.

Even if she filled one of those five-subject narrow ruled notebooks she used in high school, she'd be lucky to relieve one-tenth of the stress she experienced today. She stopped on the fifth page, released the pen from her cramped fingers and massaged her right hand with her left. She realized how tightly she had gripped her pen by the indentation of her words on the paper as she flipped from page to page.

Shannon rose to her feet and stripped down. Perhaps a shower would do her some good, or at least distract her if nothing else. She lathered her hair with the hotel shampoo, then massaged in the conditioner. It was not the quality hair product she preferred but it would have to do. What did it matter anyway? It's not like she was grooming herself for someone she cared about. She ran the floral scented soap over her body and wondered why the hotel would supply such a feminine smelling soap. Surely, they knew guys would use this as well. Whatever. What did it matter?

Shannon stood under the strong, steady stream of hot water as she wrapped herself in her own arms. She was at a loss, completely drained, no longer able to process any coherent thoughts. Inhaling the thick, steamy air, she tightened her grip and pretended Nick's arms held her, not her own. The thought made her smile for the first time since her abduction.

Earlier in the week, he had accompanied her in the shower. His skilled hands not only washed her clean, they brought unimaginable pleasure. She had been in a hurry to get ready for work that morning. When he stepped into the shower, she forgot—no, ignored—the rush she had been in moments earlier. Prior to meeting, Nick she'd never had an issue rolling out of bed, getting ready for the day and arriving at work on time. But in the past several months climbing out of bed, leaving the comfort and warmth of his arms, proved to be a nearly impossible task for her to undertake.

He'd started her rubdown using a thick, soft shower mitt. The heat from his hand seeped through the material, warming her core even more than what could be attributed to the hot spray of the shower. The suds rinsed from her breasts faster than Nick could suds them up, but he continued to work at it, slow and steady, massaging each breast. Inside a couple of minutes, she turned into a molten heap, hardly able to remind herself to breathe. The guy was good, and he was hers.

Shannon had leaned her head back until it rested on his shoulder, and pressed the palms of her hands to his hard-muscled, powerful thighs. It always amazed her how rock-hard they were while his skin felt soft against her fingertips.

Nick skimmed his warm lips over the side of her neck, sensitizing her skin further. The soft moan that escaped her lips caused his already hard shaft to press harder against the small of her back. His bare hand splayed across her stomach and pulled her tighter to him. His breath hitched.

He slid his hand between her thighs. Already aching for him, she widened her stance but knew he wouldn't take her right away. His touch told her she was in for one of his slow, controlled lovemaking sessions, the kind that always left her emotionally breathless. She'd have to push him if she wanted it any faster but couldn't decide which she wanted at the moment: slow and painstakingly pleasurable, or fast and hard with the same end result. She didn't want to think; she just wanted to feel.

Nick's skilled hands stilled for a brief moment before they left her body. She reached out to grab them but restrained herself, curious to see his next move.

He shed the shower mitt, edged away from her, placed his large warm hands on her shoulders and spun her to face him. His intense charcoal gaze darkened with each moment, boring straight into the innermost place of her soul. She stood naked before him but had never felt this fully exposed before. Any secrets she had to start with were now shared.

Unable to tear her gaze from him, she stood silent in awe of the man standing before her. He absolutely amazed her. His exterior layer was a bit rough around the edges. The wall surrounding him was strong and had been put in place years earlier, during his less than desired childhood. He'd lowered that defense for a just brief moment, months earlier, and Shannon was lucky enough to see the true man inside. A man who'd been hurt and was reluctant to trust, love, or give, yet wanted and needed to do both; give and receive. Somewhere along the line, he'd fully opened his heart to her and she for him. Shannon hadn't been prepared to love and be loved with such incalculable depth. It thrilled her, yet scared her. She'd come to realize that losing his love would be as detrimental as losing the ability to breath.

His hands clamped firmly around her waist and he hoisted her up as if she were light as a feather. Instinctively, she wrapped her legs around him and hooked her ankles just above his firm butt. Shannon gripped Nick's shoulders as one of his arms wrapped around the small of her back. The other hooked around her, higher on her back. His mouth clamped to her breast. His hot tongue scorched her taut, needy nipple, nearly driving her insane. He shifted to her other breast, his growing hunger unmistakable. Soon, he'd enter her. Raw need shot through her veins, she couldn't wait.

Whispering his name was all it took for him to reposition her and slide himself in to her wetness. Her back pressed to the shower wall, he drove into her, over and over. Shannon wove her fingers through his thick hair as his greedy mouth found hers. His all-knowing tongue fully explored her mouth as if it had never been there before, wanting to know more. She liked to push him to urgency, and worked to keep every bit of him eagerly interested. Shannon's vision blurred, her head pressed back. Every nerve ending in her body sparked and sizzled as Nick edged her into the clouds of bliss, and over the top. She pulsated around him causing him to drive harder and deeper into her before he exploded in her. His groan echoed in the shower walls as her limp body clung to him. He pinned her firmly between his heated body and the shower wall. With his face buried in the crook of her neck, his rapid, heated breath tickled her neck.

Nick pressed the palm of his hand against the shower wall, as if needing the support to stand. His arm loosened at the small of her back, indicating that she needed to unclasp her ankles. Her feet pressed to the shower floor and she hoped her weak knees would support her.

Nick reached over and shut the water off. His soft gaze captured hers as he flung a towel over her shoulders and rubbed her arms. He didn't need to say the words; she could tell by the look in his eyes he loved her. He wasn't one for using the words often, it was hard for him; but she didn't mind. She knew when he finally said the words out loud, he would mean them without reservation.

The pipes rattled, knocking Shannon out of her reverie and back into cold grim reality. She stood in the hotel shower stall by herself, water beating off her weary skin. She shut the water off and grabbed two towels off the rack, one to wrap her hair and the other for her body. She sat on the toilet seat and grabbed the pen and paper from the counter. Her heart nearly sank to her feet. It was time to write the note. She'd stash it in the bathroom someplace where housekeeping would find it and hopefully get it to Nick.

To whoever finds this note: a madman has kidnapped me, and he's been holding me since yesterday. I would be eternally grateful to you if you please see to it that this note makes its way to Detective Nick Spinelli, City of Milwaukee Police Department.

March 16th, 9:00 a.m.
Dear Nick,
It is with a heavy heart that I write this note. I am to be married today but not by choice. As you've probably figured out by now, Anna and I have been taken hostage by a crazy old man named Riordan O'Brien. He is trying to make good on an agreement made between my grandfather and Riordan's father, for an arranged marriage between him and my mother. For whatever reason unknown to me, that deal fell through and Riordan now believes it my responsibility to make good on the promise made by my family some years ago. His substantial inheritance is in jeopardy without a union between our two families. If not for the fact that Anna's life depends on my actions, I would dig in my heels and fight. But they have Anna, and I haven't seen her since about 3:00 a.m. We nearly escaped before our captors returned and separated us.

Crazed Reckoning

I have no idea how they plan to hold me after the ceremony, but know this: I will do everything in my power to escape. This is all so crazy. They're banking on the fact I won't make a stink as long as they have Anna, or that I can be bought. Evidently, there is a boatload of old family money at stake here. I guess they don't know me very well.

Nick, in the event I don't see you again, please know that I love you now and always. You are the one I wanted to grow old with. I will carry you forever in my heart, soul and spirit. Nick Spinelli, you are the strongest, most loving person I know. I will forever pray for your happiness and health.

Love, Shannon

After folding the note in half, Shannon inscribed Nick's name across the top.

Shannon pulled the towel from her head and buried her face into it to muffle her sobs. Minutes passed, yet her body still shivered. This was all so ridiculous. She couldn't help but wonder how on earth the O'Brien's thought they could get away with this. They'd have to lock her in a room forever or hold Anna's well-being dangling on a rope in front of her. Good Lord, how long did they intend to keep poor Anna? Forever? And what about Spinelli and her Uncle Bernie? That crazy old man had told her earlier that Uncle Bernie likely knew by now what had happened. Bernie would surely enlist Spinelli's help with the matter.

A knock sounded on the bathroom door.

"Get a move on in there. We'll be leaving soon," Riordan's ice-cold voice sounded through the doorway.

Shannon kept her face buried in her towel.

"Did you hear me?"

Lifting her head, Shannon fought to control her shaky voice.

"Yes."

Chapter Seven

Marsh wheeled the car out of the florist parking lot and headed back toward downtown. For lack of a better lead, they checked with the floral shop on 3rd Avenue to see if they were preparing for any weddings today.

From the back seat, Walker reported that he'd called every McGrath on the list with a landline but no response.

"Not a one?" Spinelli questioned.

"Nope."

Marsh took the 'business exit' off the highway. There didn't seem to be much business with only a couple of car dealerships and some restaurants. In minutes, they were back in the west side downtown area. The GPS had them hanging a right on Maple Street to cross the bay using a different bridge than before.

People herded into a bar on the corner. Spinelli glanced at the clock on the dashboard. It was just after 9:00 a.m. "Wow, they're piling into the bar already."

Marsh threw a quick glance at Spinelli. "You heard the lady at the florist shop, and evidently she was right. This town takes St. Patty's Day pretty seriously."

"I guess."

Spinelli shifted his gaze from one side of the street to the other. Trucks with parade floats and decorated cars lined both sides. People scurried down the sidewalks with their bag chairs in hand. He studied every person he spotted, but there were just too many people to take in as Marsh drove. Where was the deliveryman? Was he in this crowd?

As they neared the bridge, traffic slowed to a stop. The trucks with floats hung a right at the three-way intersection, just before the bridge.

Crazed Reckoning

The cars crossed the bay. As Marsh approached the bridge, Spinelli eyed the parade floats staged in the large boat ramp parking lot to his right. There had to be at lease twenty floats down there already; a mass of different shades of green surrounded them. People wore green hats, jackets, pants and shoes.

Marsh pulled up to the florist shop. Seeing the curb lined with 'No Parking' signs, Spinelli and Walker slid out of the car while Marsh stayed put in the running vehicle. Judging from the signs, and number of chairs already set up along the curb, Spinelli assumed this was the parade route.

He reached for the door handle but the door flung open before he could grab the knob. A man wearing a green hoodie stepped out of the shop and held the door for him and Walker. Spinelli eyed the man of medium height and build who held a fist full of green carnations in front of him. It blocked the view of his face, but Spinelli was able to catch a glimpse of long blond hair protruding out from under the hood of the man's sweatshirt. *Not him. Not the deliveryman.*

Spinelli and Walker made their way to the checkout counter and got in line. An older gentleman, wearing a white apron covered with tiny green clovers, worked behind the counter. He gave instructions on the care for a Shamrock plant to the customer opposite the counter of him. The customer nodded then followed-up with questions about watering and filtered light. Spinelli raked his hand over his face. The exchange was taking them forever. *For crissake, buddy, it's just a plant. Just throw it in a corner and water the stupid thing.* Walker shot Spinelli a sideways glance causing him to wonder if he'd just said that out loud.

The customer paid for his plant and headed out the door. The next person stepped up to the counter. He wore a long green smock with green and white striped tights and clunky black boots with gold buckles on the sides. Spinelli fought the urge to roll his eyes.

The man working the counter smiled, "What can I do for you today, Tim?"

"I guess my wife ordered a bouquet for her mother."

"Oh, okay, let me take a look."

The shop worker spun on his heel and looked through the glass cooler doors at dozens of arrangements. Scanning each cooler from top to bottom, the worker located what he needed near the bottom of the second cooler. The old man groaned as he sluggishly squatted and grabbed the vase full of green carnations accented with a large green bow.

The man slowly stood before he limped back to the counter. Setting the floral arrangement on the counter, he punched the buttons on the outdated cash register. He smiled as he handed Tim his change. "Patricia will like these. How's she doing with her new hip?"

"She's actually doing pretty well. We're so glad she agreed to do her rehab at the Center rather than at home with us. At first, she fought us tooth and nail. No way would she go to the 'old folk's home' for rehab. Thank heavens she did because she wouldn't be as far along as she is without professional help."

The shop worker nodded. "We ran into a similar issue with my wife's aunt. They think we'll leave them in the nursing home forever once we get them in there."

Spinelli blew out an exaggerated sigh. *Would they just shut up already?*

The customer turned, glanced at Spinelli, grabbed his floral arrangement and walked away. Spinelli's cheeks heated. In the past, he'd been physically attacked more times than he could count. Knives and guns had been pulled on him, but not one of those instances stressed him out more than this very moment. Knowing Shannon and Anna's abductors would likely not physically hurt them didn't help ease his anxiety. He knew the emotional trauma could be life changing, and the longer it went on the more severe the impact. Adrenaline shot through his veins. Shannon's emotional health depended on him, just like nearly three months ago when the drug dealer, Loukas the Greek, kidnapped her. Though she survived that incident with little impact, Spinelli couldn't help but wonder how many more times she could undergo such ordeals without cracking.

Her strength brought some assurance to him. With her soft delicate features, she didn't look strong on the outside, but on the inside, she was tough as nails. Her strength was just one of the many things he had grown to love about her. At this very moment, he never felt so powerless, hopeless and scared in all his life. Shannon would soon be coerced into marrying someone she didn't love. He should have married her the day he met her. Deep down he knew they were soul mates, and even with their rocky start, she knew it too. If they were married already, this wouldn't be happening.

Walker grabbed a shamrock plant off the rack next to the counter. "We'll take one of these," he said and he reached for his wallet. He fully exposed his badge as he pulled out some cash to pay for the plant.

The store clerk's gaze fixed on the badge.

Walker cleared his throat. "Is your shop doing any weddings today?

The clerk's slow-moving gaze reached Walker's. "No, none today."

"Do you know the McGrath family?"

Pulling a frown, the clerk shifted his puzzled gaze from Walker to Spinelli and then back to Walker. "Yes, I know some McGrath's from up north, but not well. They've done business here on occasion."

Spinelli held the picture of the McGrath they obtained from the resort in front of the clerk's eyes. "Do you know this man?"

Pushing his glasses into place, the man leaned forward and eyed the photo for a few seconds before he shook his head. "No, but anyone and everyone who's Irish, and even those who aren't, will be downtown today for the Saint Patrick's Day parade." The man let out a chuckle. "The Saint Patty's Day celebration is like Christmas in March to the people in this county." The man's smile widened. "Oddly, most of them will be too hung-over tomorrow to enjoy the real Saint Patty's Day. I guess it's good we always hold the parade on the Saturday nearest the actual holiday, it gives most people a day to recuperate before returning to work on Monday."

"What time does the parade start?" Spinelli asked.

The clerk glanced at his watch, "In just over an hour and a half at11:00, but people are already filtering into the downtown area. I'm sure the bars are likely packed and serving green beer."

Seriously, people are drinking already. It was no secret it would be hard enough to find Shannon and Anna in unfamiliar territory, but now they had to deal with an enormous influx of people. To make matters even worse, add alcohol to the mix. "It looked like the floats were lining up across the bay, at the boat ramp. Is that where they officially start?"

"Yes."

"What is the route?"

The man pointed out the window toward the bridge over which they'd just driven. "The parade will cross the bridge and then turn down Third Avenue here and go about five blocks."

"That's it? Just five blocks?"

The clerk smiled. "Well, that pretty much covers the downtown."

Spinelli nodded. "I see."

Noting the line of customers building behind them, Spinelli thanked the man for his time as Walker grabbed his Shamrock plant off the counter.

Marsh still waited at the curb for them. Spinelli glanced down the street before climbing into the car. In the short amount of time they'd been in the florist shop, the number of chairs and people on the curb had at least doubled.

"Well?" Marsh asked when they climbed into the car.

"No weddings for this shop. And it appears everyone in the county will be in Sturgeon Bay for the parade today," Spinelli replied.

"I guess that's good news for us. Our delivery man, Mr. McGrath, will be at our fingertips—somewhere in this downtown area."

Spinelli pointed out the windshield. Everyone and their brother wore green. Lucky for them, a number of people wore sweatshirts with their names depicted on the back. That would narrow the search some, providing the guy still wore his 'McGrath' hoodie. "We should find a place to park, each take a block or two, and start combing the area for the delivery man."

Marsh signaled and pulled into traffic.

Spinelli saw Marsh eyeing Walker's Shamrock plant through the rearview mirror. He knew without doubt what was about to happen. Marsh cleared his throat. *Yep, here it comes.*

"I see you have one of those Shamrock plants," Marsh stated as if Walker didn't already know.

Walker sighed before answering, "Yeah."

"You know, those make great houseplants. For the most part, they're low maintenance. You don't even have to water them weekly. Every 10 to 14 days should do the trick. I've heard, though, that every couple of months you have to flush them to remove the salts from the soil. That could be a pain to deal with, I guess."

Marsh flipped his blinker on and hung a right. Spinelli pointed at the public parking sign that lay just ahead. Excellent. Now they could park and separate; he wouldn't have to hear any more of Marsh's useless information about Shamrock plants. Though Marsh irritated the heck out of him at times, Spinelli found himself equally amazed by how Marsh's mind worked. It was like he had a photographic memory. Marsh only had to read or see something once and it seemed embedded in his mind forever, in its entirety. Spinelli wondered if Marsh's brain ever hurt from storing tons of useless information like the care of Shamrock plants and tropical fish or the history and purpose of all the ancient gods.

Marsh exited the full parking lot.

Spinelli knew what this meant. He and Walker would have to endure more rambling about the Shamrock plant until they found a place to park. He kept his eyes peeled for a spot.

Marsh glanced back at Walker who looked like he already regretted his purchase. "And just so you know, Shamrocks should have purified or distilled water, not tap water."

"Okay, I'm on it, no need to worry," Walker replied, unable to hide the annoyance in his voice.

"Also, did you know that Shamrocks go into dormancy?"

"No, can't say I did."

"During that time, you shouldn't water or fertilize them at all. I guess you are supposed to store them in a dark cool place. When they start developing new shoots, you can put them back into an area with sunshine and resume watering them."

"Good to know."

Spinelli was sure Walker wanted to chuck the plant out the window by now. In fact, he probably wanted to jump out the window as well.

Marsh hung a left on Fifth Avenue, and then another immediate left.

"There's a spot," Spinelli said as he pointed up ahead. "Park there and we'll walk to the downtown area."

Spinelli slid out of the car and yanked up the zipper on his jacket. The unseasonably cold air had not warmed at all since the early morning hours.

They crossed over Fourth Avenue, then onto Third Avenue. Both directions were crowded with people, dressed in every shade of green imaginable, setting up their lawn chairs along the curb before they disappeared into the shops, restaurants and bars lining the street.

Spinelli sent Marsh to the south and he and Walker headed north, on opposite sides of the street, to search for their deliveryman. Spinelli intently eyed every passerby. McGrath had to be in the area; he just had to be.

Children wore little leprechaun hats, flashing shamrock pins and numerous other Saint Patty's Day accessories. Their little faces beamed with excitement. Spinelli passed by some kids standing in line at a face-painting booth. Two teenaged girls shivered while they painted shamrocks and rainbows on the kids' cheeks.

Spinelli's feet carried him quickly as he popped in and out of stores along his path but found mostly women and children meandering about. His chest constricted. He was coming up empty on his search for McGrath. Time was of the essence. He needed to catch a break and would give anything for the slightest bit of information. Even if that meant cutting a deal with the devil himself.

Music echoed from up the street, growing clearer and louder with each step Spinelli took as he neared the end of the downtown district. He slipped into the bar near the end of the block. With what he'd already seen on this celebratory Saint Patty's Day weekend, it didn't surprise him that the bar was already jam-packed full of people drinking green beer and dancing to the DJ's music. One usually encountered this kind of scene at 10:00 at night, not before 10:00 a.m. Easing his way through the crowd, he closely eyed every man in his path. Though nearly everyone wore something green, no one had apparel with their names printed on the back like he'd seen earlier in the day.

"Hey, buddy!" the young male bartender yelled from behind the bar, catching Spinelli's attention.

"Yeah," Spinelli replied as he stepped closer to the man.

"Are you looking for someone?"

"As a matter of fact, I am. I'm looking for McGrath."

"Which one?"

"I'm not sure of his first name but here's a picture of him," Spinelli replied as he handed the photo of McGrath to the young man.

The bartender eyed the picture for a minute, looking as though he debated whether or not to fess up to knowing the man. "Honestly, I know some of the McGrath's but I'm not sure which one this is. It is likely he's in town today. I would imagine they'll all be in the parade."

"In the parade?"

The bartender pulled a frown. "Yep, all the Irish clans in the county will be in the parade. Today is their day," he said in a tone, matching the expression on his face, which made Spinelli feel stupid for even asking.

"All the Irish clans?"

"Yes, all the Irish clans: the O'Hern's, O'Reilly's, Clarke's, Hogan's, Kennedy's, McGinnis' and your McGrath's will all be represented in the parade today. You'll be able to distinguish them by the names on their shirts or sweatshirts."

Spinelli took the picture of McGrath back from the bartender and thanked him for the information. Knowing he needed to gather up Walker and Marsh and head over to the boat ramp parking lot on the other side of the bay, he worked his way back through the crowd toward the front door.

A group of young ladies blocked the exit. Like everyone else, they dressed in green attire. The tall, pretty girl with pitch-black hair stepped toward him. Her cheeks glistened with gold specks dabbled over a painted four-leaf clover. The model-grade woman gave him a onceover and edged closer as her friends stood smiling in the background. She pulled several strands of green beads over her head and slid them over his before she pressed her soft lips to his cheek. Her warm breath brushed by his ear. "You need a little color of the day. Why don't you stay here and party with us?" she asked before she edged back and batted her large brown eyes lined with long thick lashes. Her warm hands still rested on his chest. He glanced beyond her to find the entire group of ladies watching him curiously. They looked like a friendly bunch about to embark on a fun, party-filled day.

Pre-Shannon, he would have considered her offer. Now, all he had on his mind was locating his very own Irish sweetheart. "Thanks for the invite but unfortunately I have somewhere else I need to be right now."

The model tilted her head to the side and flashed him a wink. "If you change your mind, we'll be downtown all day." Dropping her hands to her sides, she stepped back so he could pass through.

Once outside, Spinelli texted Walker and Marsh to meet him at the car. Spinelli hurried, fighting the throng of Saint Patrick's Day celebrators along the way. The thickness of the crowd reminded him of the Macy's Thanksgiving Day Parade he'd seen on television but on a small-town scale.

Quickly rounding the building on the corner of Third and Louisiana Street, Spinelli nearly bumped into a couple older women. He reached out and grabbed one woman's shoulders as she rocked back on her heels. The amount of pull told him he would have caused her to fall if he hadn't grabbed her quickly. He steadied her before he dropped his hands to his sides. "I'm sorry, ma'am."

Her glistening green eyes matched her bright green scarf and hat. "Where's the fire, handsome?" she asked with a giggle.

He returned her warm smile. "Nowhere, I should have been paying attention to where I was going."

"Oh, that's okay. The near-fall was worth it just to feel the strong hands of a handsome fella for a moment. In fact, why don't you go back around the corner and we'll give it another whirl?"

"June, my word," the other woman interjected.

Spinelli didn't need to turn his head to see the woman's friend blushed. The air temperature rose five degrees from the heat emitting from her pores.

"Oh, simmer down Germaine. You're just jealous his hands weren't on you," June replied, her gaze never leaving Spinelli as she ran the length of him. "Nice beads, but you need a bit more color for today," June said as she reached into her large handbag. She pulled out a green crocheted leprechaun hat with a black band and gold buckle. It even had flaps to go over his ears and long braided strings to tie under his chin. Under normal circumstances, he wouldn't be caught dead in this hat. Something about her sassy, grandmotherly nature made him lean forward so she could fasten it to his head. Though he must have looked utterly ridiculous, it did warm his head against the cold gusty wind.

June eyed him proudly. "You know, I have a daughter about your age and she's meeting us down here in a little while."

"For heaven's sake, June."

June's head spun in Germaine's direction. "What? I'm just asking this nice handsome young man if he'd like to join us for the parade." With a shake of her head, June's gaze returned to Spinelli. "I don't know how she and I came from the same set of parents. I've told her for years she needs to loosen up a bit." June stepped closer to him as though she wanted to tell him something privately. He leaned toward her. "I think she's adopted."

Spinelli chuckled and glanced at Germaine in time to catch her eye-roll.

If it weren't for the awful day he was having, and his need to find Shannon and Anna, he'd consider June's offer to spend some time with her and her sister. They reminded him of Shannon's cute little old neighbors, the spry little twins, who'd turned ninety this past Valentine's Day. One was just a little pistol and the other was as practical as the day is long. The two women before him were the next generation's version of Sally and Sarah.

His mind revisited the offer from the model-like woman at the bar. If he had his choice, and had time today, he'd choose to spend his day with the ladies standing before him now. Did he really just think that? He'd spend his day with two seventy-some year old ladies versus the twenty-some year old model and her friends. Oh, how times have changed.

"Ladies, it was a pleasure, and if I didn't have somewhere else to be I would love to watch the parade with you. Enjoy your day," Spinelli said as he slipped by them and headed toward the car.

He'd just about reached Fourth Avenue when he noticed Walker and Marsh already waiting for him.

As Spinelli slid into the passenger seat, Marsh's curious gaze fixed on him. "What in the hell are you wearing? Are you supposed to be some sort of six-foot-tall leprechaun?"

Remembering the hat he wore, Spinelli reached up and pulled it from his head. "It's a long story."

"Well, what about the beads? What did you have to do for those while Walker and I were out looking for the delivery guy, and Shannon and Anna?" Marsh asked in a teasing tone.

Spinelli wasn't in the mood for Marsh's alleged humor. Marsh never seemed to know when to zip his lips. "How about you just never mind what happened to me and drive us over to the boat ramp where they're staging the floats for the parade. According to the bartender I talked to, the McGrath's will be in the parade."

Marsh put the car in gear and pulled into traffic. Spinelli hoped to get across the bridge before the city closed it to traffic for the parade. As they crossed, he glanced over toward the boat ramp parking lot filled with floats. Just over the bridge, Marsh hung a left and then another left into the parking lot. He pulled into one of the few remaining stalls available and cut the engine.

Spinelli grabbed his new hat and flung his door open.

Marsh glanced at him and cocked a brow. "You can't possibly be serious?"

"What?"

"You're actually going to wear that ridiculous hat?"

"It's warm, I like it, and it will help me fit in with the crowd. Now, let's find the McGrath's."

Spinelli, Walker and Marsh entered the endless sea of green. First, they spotted the O'Hern clan, a loud and rowdy bunch, all dressed in green from head to toe. Their matching green hooded sweatshirts had 'O'Hern Clan' stamped on the back and almost all of them clenched a green solo cup in their hand. Spinelli glanced at his watch. Nearly 10:00 a.m. and this group was partying like they'd been at it for a while.

A young woman with a green afro wig caught his gaze. "Nice hat."

"Thank you. Say, do you know where we can find the McGrath Clan?"

Her nose wrinkled and dark eyes oozed with competitiveness. "Those losers" We're so kicking their asses in the float contest this year!" The gold bells on her shoes jingled as she shifted her feet in the direction of the O'Hern float.

Spinelli glanced in that direction as well. Their float consisted of one of those large inflatable leprechauns and a pot of gold with a rainbow shooting out of it. The leprechaun, at least eight feet tall, stood next to a plush velvet covered chair. It sat on a platform a bit higher than the rest of the simple green chairs on the flatbed trailer. It reminded him of the one he sat on while playing Santa Claus at the mall, only this chair was green rather than red. He supposed the chair was meant for the elder O'Hern.

Long streamers attached to shiny gold posts whipped in the breeze. Green and white balloons, some shaped like shamrocks, lined several arches stretching from one side to the other of the float. He was surprised to see the balloons holding up in the frigid temperature.

Irish music blared from the truck attached to the trailer. The tap of a keg peeked out from under a tarp on the bed of the truck. Only in small town Wisconsin could someone siphon from a keg on the back of a pickup truck on public property.

Spinelli nodded at the woman. "Your float looks good, I'm sure you'll win."

The woman's smile stretched from ear to ear. "Thanks. Hmm, let's see, the McGrath's are down there, second or third from the end of the lineup," the woman replied as she pointed and craned her neck to glance around Walker.

"Great, thanks for your help."

Walker spun to head in the direction of the McGrath's but the girl they spoke with grabbed his arm. "Wait," she said as she pulled a pair of green shamrock glasses from the pouch on her sweatshirt and handed them to Walker. Walker reluctantly took them from her and put them on as Marsh tried to stifle his chuckle. "And just what are you laughing at, mister?" she asked Marsh as she pulled the green clown-looking wig from her head and secured it onto his. "You can't be walking around here without any Saint Patty's Day attire. That just wouldn't be right."

Excellent, now Spinelli had company. And though he already wore a leprechaun hat and green beads, the lady evidently felt the need to add to his wardrobe as well as she pulled the feathery green boa wrap from around her neck and wrapped it around him. Though he looked even more ridiculous, he couldn't say it bothered him. He was willing to do whatever it took to find McGrath so he could find Shannon and Anna.

"There, that's better," the woman uttered as she spun on her heel and headed back toward her clan.

It didn't take but a minute to find the McGrath Clan, all dressed in their matching green zip-up hoodies. There looked to be fifteen to twenty McGrath's putting the finishing touches on their float. It looked good.

The O'Herns would have a run for their money.

Spinelli, Walker and Marsh eyed the four adult men in the clan. They all resembled the man in the photo.

Walker pulled his green glasses from his face and took another look at the photo he had of the deliveryman. "That's him, over there standing at the back of the float," Walker said as he pointed at the man."

They walked over to the back of the float. "Excuse me," Walker said, drawing the man's attention.

"Yeah?"

"We're looking for a friend of ours and hope you can help us out."

The guy jumped down from the float. "Sure, who are you looking for?"

"Did you deliver an envelope to a waitress this morning at the Harbor Resort Restaurant?"

The man shifted his nervous gaze among them. The internal debate he held in regard to tell the truth or not became transparent.

"Yes."

"How did you obtain the envelope?"

McGrath stuffed his hands into his pockets. "Some old man I don't know pulled me aside in the lobby and handed me one hundred bucks. He asked me to make sure the waitress got the envelope right away so she could give it to some guy named Spinelli who was in the restaurant." McGrath shrugged. "I just did it. I didn't think much about it. It was easy money."

"Do you know if the person who gave you the envelope is staying at the resort?"

"I didn't ask. Is he in some sort of trouble?"

"Possibly," Walker replied as he pulled his wallet from his pocket and flashed his detective badge at the man.

McGrath sighed. "I knew it was too good to be true. Am I in trouble?"

"Not really, but we do need help finding this guy. He may be holding a friend of ours."

The blood drained from McGrath's face.

Spinelli and Marsh listened as Walker continued to question McGrath.

"Can you tell us exactly what happened this morning?"

McGrath stood silent for a moment and looked as though he was trying to get his thoughts in order. "Shortly before 6:00 this morning, I went into the lobby to see if they would let me check in early. My whole family is staying there tonight so we don't have to drive home after partying all day. They let me check in and I went upstairs to throw my stuff in the room. I came back down right away to meet my brothers for breakfast downtown at 6:00. An old guy, standing in the corner of the reception area, motioned to me as I entered the lobby. He asked if I could help him with something. I agreed, so he handed me the money and the envelope, and that was all there was to the exchange." McGrath shifted his gaze among them again and before anyone else could speak he continued, "I was in such a hurry to meet my brothers, I really just didn't give it any thought."

"Dammit," Spinelli uttered, "he was right at our fingertips."

Walker turned his attention back to McGrath, "Can you describe the man at all?"

"He has short white hair. I'd say he's in his mid-sixties. He's at least my height. The only detail I really noticed about him was his eyes."

"What about his eyes?" Walker asked.

McGrath's face scrunched. "They seemed so … I don't know, I guess hollow."

"Hollow?"

"You know, empty or cold. Again, I was in such a hurry I didn't worry about it. Plus I was more focused on the midget."

"The midget?"

"I'm sorry, I mean little person."

Spinelli knew he didn't dare risk a glance at Marsh at this point. He didn't, in any way, shape or form, want to give Marsh any reason to make some sort of uncouth comments about little people.

Walker kept his expression in check as he usually did. "So the old man was with a little person?"

"I don't know if they were together, but I couldn't help but notice him standing nearby and watching us. It just seemed peculiar to me."

"Peculiar?"

"Well, you know, being Saint Patrick's Day weekend and all. I couldn't help but picture him in a green velvet suit, riding on one of the floats. I suspected the O'Herns brought him in for their float." McGrath shook his head. "I swear they'll stop at nothing to win the competition."

A beat of silence passed.

"Sorry, I can't help what I pictured," McGrath added as if guilt swept through him for his simple-minded thought about the little person. "But on a good note, if they are together they should be easy for you to find," McGrath offered in desperation.

Spinelli knew Walker and Marsh were of like mind. They knew what McGrath meant.

Walker handed McGrath his card, asked him to call if he saw the man who gave him the envelope or the little person, and thanked him for his time.

Spinelli's heart raced as they piled into the car and headed back to the resort. He was one step closer to finding Shannon and Anna. They were at the resort; he could feel it in his bones. Though he was excited, he wanted to kick himself for wasting so much time already, when the captors had been right at his fingertips.

They piled into the car and Marsh speedily drove them back to the hotel. Leaping from the car, Spinelli high-tailed it to the receptionist desk and rang the bell for service. The clerk poked her head around the corner and held her index finger in the air. "I'll be right with you."

A moment later, she resurfaced. "How can I help you?"

Spinelli went with what he had, "We're looking for a gray-haired man in his sixties who may have checked in with a little person. Have you seen anyone fitting this description?"

The woman nodded.

"Did they check in with anyone else?"

She shook her head.

He leaned forward, rested his elbows on the counter and flashed his lady-killer grin. The grin that usually got him whatever he wanted from the opposite sex. "Can you tell me what room they are in?"

Her headshake came slow, and her quick glance to the security camera told Spinelli it wouldn't take much more to get what he wanted from this woman. "I understand. One other thing though, I seem to have lost my room keycard. Can I get a new one?" he asked for the benefit of the audio that likely came along with the security camera system.

"Sure, no problem. I just need your driver's license so I can find you in the system."

Spinelli lifted his elbows off the counter, stood up straight and pulled his wallet from his pocket. Holding it low between him and the counter, out of view of the camera, he pulled his license from it, along with the folded fifty-dollar bill he always stashed for emergency purposes. He carefully set the license onto the counter and slid it over to her with the bill tucked securely beneath it. With a knowing smile, she reached over, pressed her fingers to the license and continued to slide it in her direction. Judging from her experience, Spinelli guessed she'd helped a few jealous lovers from time to time.

As her fingers danced across the keyboard to program a new keycard for him, he inquired about the location of the hotel gym. She finished with the card, pulled a hotel map from the stack next to her and placed it on the counter in front of him. "You are here and the gym is here," she said as she quickly circled a room number and handed him the map.

"Thank you."

"No problem, have a good day."

They stepped away from the desk, and Spinelli glanced at the map. Adrenaline shot through his veins. The room number the clerk circled had to be a mistake.

"What is it?" Marsh asked as he took the map from Spinelli's hand. "For crissake, un-freaking believable."

Spinelli shot to the stairs. He sprinted up the steps two at a time, and then he ran down the hall stopping at the suite right next to his room. She'd been in the suite right next to him the entire time.

Walker threw himself between Spinelli and the door. "Wait."

Walker pressed his ear to the door. "It's quiet."

Spinelli feared he was too late and the girls weren't there any longer.

Walker knocked and they all stepped out of the peephole view hoping someone would actually open the door.

Nothing.

Walker knocked again. This time they heard a masculine groan. They paused, and another groan sounded, clearly not that of a woman.

Spinelli glanced down the hall in both directions. Seeing no one, he drew his weapon, slipped the keycard into the slot and pushed his way through the door with Walker and Marsh in tow. They slipped through the narrow kitchenette and into the living room space to find an old gray-haired man and little person gagged and bound together, back-to-back in kitchen chairs.

He let Walker deal with them as he and Marsh checked the two bedrooms attached to the suite. Spinelli's heart plummeted into his stomach. Empty. Hardly able to think, he could hear Walker talking to the men but couldn't process what they said now that Walker had removed their gags. For security purposes, Walker kept the men tied up.

Spinelli's phone buzzed, snapping him back into reality. He pulled it from his hip and glanced at the screen. Bernie.

"Spinelli here."

"Hey Nick, it's Bernie. Davin and I are in the hotel lobby. Where are you guys?"

"We're here, Suite 342. Come on up," Spinelli replied. He'd fill Bernie in on what little he knew when he got here.

Walker's words came clearer now. He heard him ask the men about Shannon and Anna's whereabouts. They denied knowing anything about the women.

The old man glanced in Spinelli's direction and smirked. Instinctively, Spinelli leapt toward him but Marsh blocked his path before he could wring the old man's neck. Glancing around Marsh, he caught a glimpse of the man's eyes. He now understood what McGrath had meant. Evil oozed from the old man's glare. Spinelli had seen that look before, countless times, in the eyes of killers he'd arrested. Sharp pains shot through his ears as a result of his knotted jaw. Shannon and Anna had been in this man's hands, and now they were nowhere to be found.

"Dammit, Riordan, what have you done? Where is she?" Bernie's stern yet agitated voice sounded as he rounded the kitchenette toward the old man. Bernie's furious eyes told of his intention.

"I don't have her, you reneging hypocrite," Riordan yelled as he squirmed to free himself from the chair, but the ropes bound him tightly.

Walker stepped into Bernie's path and held his hand up. "Everybody just stop!"

Bernie took another step.

"Stop, I said." Walker didn't mess around. There was work to be done here and no time for tempers.

Bernie stopped and looked back. All eyes drifted in the same direction. "Davin, get in here, you little chicken shit."

Riordan growled something Spinelli couldn't quite make out but chose to ignore him. Curiosity flooded him. He needed to see the man Shannon was bound to marry today. What would he look like, sound like and act like? Would he have treated her decently, had they actually married? A lump the size of a golf ball formed in his throat as the last question passed through his mind.

"Davin," Bernie snapped again.

Keeping his eyes glued to the entryway, Spinelli swallowed hard to prepare himself for the man about to enter.

Davin rounded the corner of the kitchenette, stopped and shifted his gaze until it landed on Riordan, his father. Spinelli studied the small man with bright blue eyes and thick wavy red hair before he glanced back at the little person tied to the chair. *Twins, identical twins.*

Everything suddenly made sense. They'd sent Davin to Bernie as a diversion, so his twin could marry Shannon before anyone knew what happened. Another question crossed Spinelli's mind. Was the man standing by the kitchenette really Davin O'Brien or was he the man bound to the chair? Other than Davin, his nameless twin and his dad, who would know which one was which? Would Bernie know? The look on Bernie's face as he looked between the twins told Spinelli he couldn't tell either. At this point, it didn't really matter. They couldn't have a wedding without a bride. Where on earth were Shannon and Anna, and why were Riordan and one of the twins now tied up?

"This is your fault, Davin. If you were any kind of man, we wouldn't be here," Riordan yelled, giving the real Davin away.

Davin's shoulders slumped. "Yes, I know. I'm always a disappointment. You've made that quite clear on more than one occasion."

Davin stepped toward Spinelli, his gaze serious. "Mr. Spinelli, honestly, I came here to try to cut a deal with Bernie and Shannon in hopes to secure my family's inheritance. I have no idea where she and her friend are at the moment. However, there is absolutely no doubt in my mind that my father and Collin are behind their disappearance. They're crazy and out of control over this whole inheritance thing. I'm sick of it and I'm done with them."

Spinelli believed him.

"Why you useless little …" Riordan stared.

Spinelli lunged toward Riordan, his hands gripped the arms of his chair, his face only inches in front of Riordan's. "Shut up! The only thing I want to hear out of your mouth right now is information in regard to Shannon and Anna's whereabouts!"

The room fell silent as Spinelli and Riordan continued the stare-down. Spinelli could feel Walker's presence at his side but he didn't say a word. He stayed close, likely to keep him from wringing the old man's neck.

Riordan's blue eyes darkened with each passing moment. There was no fear in Riordan's eyes as there should be for a man bound to a chair, facing two counts of kidnapping. He shared a room with three detectives, and a family member who'd just pointed the finger at him. It was clear by his behavior, this man was as crazy as they came.

Riordan's stone-cold gaze didn't waver. Spinelli knew he'd stick to his story. Perhaps they could break Collin.

Chapter Eight

Shannon and Anna sat at the small kitchen table in the condo they'd been brought to nearly an hour earlier. The woman with the gun eyed them through the holes on the glittery green mask she wore as she sat on a leather chair near the fireplace. She kept her unwavering gaze on them as they ate the omelets and fruit the woman had ordered for them via room service.

Trusting the food hadn't been tampered with since it came from the resort's restaurant, Shannon and Anna willingly accepted the meal. Neither had eaten anything since lunch the prior day.

As she ate, Shannon's gaze shifted about the room and searched for an escape route. They weren't far from the door but both she and Anna had one wrist cuffed to a decorative loop on the leg of the heavy wrought iron table. She doubted they could break the leg off the table or escape carrying the table out with them.

On a good note, she was with Anna once again. As it turned out, they were never that far apart from one another. Anna had simply been moved to the other bedroom in the suite. Shannon could tell by Anna's surprised reaction when they were reunited that Anna also had no idea of Shannon's close proximity.

As Shannon sipped her orange juice, she recalled the priceless look in Riordan's eyes as the new captors walked her and Anna past him, toward the exit. The fierce rage in his glare was nothing like Shannon had ever seen before, and in her line of work, she'd seen some pretty nasty stares. Losing the inner battle she fought as she blew by Riordan, Shannon returned his stare with a self-satisfied, victorious one of her own. It sent him on a tirade, growling through his gag and bouncing in

89

Valerie J. Clarizio

his chair like a toddler throwing a temper tantrum as he tried to wriggle his way free. Glad the crazy old man was bound tightly to that kitchen chair, he would have likely killed one, if not all of them, if he'd been free. Oddly, his son sat quietly, with not a peep or reaction from him. Perhaps he felt his father fussed enough for the both of them.

Shannon didn't know where her new abductors would take her or what they wanted from her and Anna. She was glad to leave the confines of Riordan and thrilled to know she would likely not be wedding his son. But still, why were these ladies stealing her and Anna away from Riordan?

The woman with the gun shifted in her chair. Shannon fixed her attention on the lady as she lifted her arm until it rested on the chair's wide armrest. Her grip remained in place on the butt of the gun, and her index finger rested near the trigger. The woman's other hand lay on the opposite armrest. Her drumming fingers annoyed the heck out of Shannon, but since the lady held a gun, Shannon thought twice about saying anything.

The woman's wrinkled hands and gray hair peeking out from under her lime-green wig, gave away her age. Shannon guessed she was in her mid-sixties. But the other captor, the woman who had helped bring them to their new holding-place, seemed younger. She too wore a plastic green mask fastened to her face and sported a green wig.

Shannon shifted in her chair. Her ribs hurt where the woman had pressed the barrel of the gun as they walked out of the Harbor Resort in Sturgeon Bay with their arms slung around each other. Anna and the other woman had followed closely behind them, Anna at gunpoint as well.

How had they been kidnapped twice in less than a twenty-four period? So much for the luck of the Irish during this Saint Patrick's Day weekend. Perhaps that would change tomorrow, on Saint Patrick's Day. She could only hope.

Forking another mouthful of her omelet, she wondered again why they wanted her and Anna, and how they knew where to find them. At least she understood the motive of her other captors, but these two had not yet given any hint as to who they were and what they planned on doing with her and Anna. They had refused to answer any questions she

90

and Anna asked on their twenty-minute ride up to Egg Harbor.

Shannon thought about Nick. Where was he? How had he not yet located her? She sighed. Good grief, she couldn't blame him. This wasn't his fault. If she had listened to him in the first place, she wouldn't be in this predicament, would she? Would their captors have abducted them elsewhere?

The front door to the condo opened and the younger woman stepped through, her mask and wig still in place. How convenient nobody would find it peculiar they wore costumes.

Shannon wondered why this holiday was so utterly important to everyone in Door County. She didn't recall any massive group of Irish settlers in this particular area. She did remember historical information about Belgian settlers in Door County, even some German and Norwegian settlers. Evidently, there must have been some Irish immigrants, though. Perhaps Saint Patrick's Day, or March in general, was readily welcomed by the residents here after the harsh winter months. *Good grief, why am I thinking about this now? Who cares?*

The young woman blew by their table without a glance before she settled into a chair opposite side the older lady. She opened the laptop on the oval cocktail table and powered it up before she spoke to the other woman. "They say it shouldn't be much longer. He'll be dead soon, and we'll be able to put this all behind us."

The older woman blew out an exaggerated sigh as she leaned forward in her chair. "Finally, my revenge. What I'd give to see the look on the arse's face when his world comes crumbling down. Years, I've waited years for this moment."

The fork shook in Shannon's hand. Who were they talking about? Who would be dead soon? Anna's eyes shared the same concern. Selfishly, Shannon found some comfort that the abductors referred to the soon-to-be-dead person as a male. But what part did she and Anna play in this whole thing?

* * * *

Walker continued to interrogate Riordan and Collin as Spinelli and Marsh searched the first bedroom, which closely resembled his room next door. He must have mentally kicked himself a thousand times.

She'd been right next to him this entire time. His chest constricted at the mere thought of how scared she had probably been during this whole ordeal. Though her strength brought a smidgen of comfort to him, she'd been through so much already these past several months he worried how much more she could take. At least she had Anna with her, or so he hoped.

Spinelli's gaze zoned in on the wedding dress that lay over the back of the small leather chair facing the fireplace. He held the hanger in the air. Unease curled in his stomach at the thought of what nearly happened to Shannon today. A wave of anxiety, from the realization he hadn't a clue what may be happening to her presently, followed the agonizing unease.

"What do you have there?" Marsh asked.

Spinelli shot a glance over his shoulder before he turned to face Marsh with the wedding dress draped over his arm. "A wedding dress." The words had come hard through his closing throat. Spinelli spun and carelessly tossed the dress back over the chair. It didn't matter if it wrinkled or fell to the floor. Shannon wouldn't need that dress. If he had his way, she would need a white dress of her own choosing in the very near future.

Realigning his thoughts, he looked back at Marsh. "Find anything?"

"Yes," Marsh replied as he glanced down at his latex gloved hand. With a sober look, his arm extended toward Spinelli. "I found this in the bathroom, tucked under the counter by the spare towels."

Spinelli's palm perspired as he took the note from Marsh. It took only a split second for him to recognize Shannon's penmanship.

Focusing on the paper, Spinelli scanned the words. Shannon started the letter by asking the finder to forward the letter to him. She continued on to identify her abductor as Riordan and give a brief explanation for the abduction. Renewed anger shot through his veins with the speed of light.

Anxiety soon jockeyed for position with the anger, as Spinelli learned from Shannon's letter that she and Anna had been separated. All this time, he'd found a small level of comfort knowing they had each other. Now that smidgeon of comfort was ripped from him.

Spinelli swiped his sweaty palm against his thigh and shot Marsh a quick glance before returning his gaze back to the letter. A small sense of pride unfolded within him when Shannon told of the near escape and her will to flee this mess altogether. Shannon was the classic example of 'looks can be deceiving.' Her small frame and fine features made her appear soft and gentle, perhaps even frail. But her family and close friends knew better. She had a strong will and character that gave her inconceivable strength. Spinelli knew they'd have their hands full; she'd never yield to anyone.

The last paragraph of the letter proved to be the most difficult to read. Shannon's words, written with such steadfast conviction, nearly leaped off the paper for the whole world to see. He knew before reading the letter she loved him but to see the words written in such a way. It bore into the deepest depth of his soul and penetrated a layer he never knew existed until this very moment.

Shannon's final words sifted through his mind again.

Please know that I love you now and always. You are the one I wanted to grow old with. I will carry you forever in my heart, soul and spirit. Nick Spinelli, you are the strongest, most loving person I know. I will forever pray for your happiness and health.

She was in the hands of a madman, and worried about praying for him rather than herself. Shannon was the most unselfish, loving, and caring person he'd ever met. He had to find her, he had to make her his, if it was the last thing he ever did. If it took the very breath from his body, it would be worth it because life without her meant nothing.

He stared at the letter in his shaky, sweaty hand, his gaze glued to the paper. The words blurred. Unable to bear the thought of Marsh, of all people, catching a glimpse of his teary eyes, he blinked rapidly and kept them fixed on the black mass of words in front of him. Marsh's lack of couth was not what he needed right now.

The warmth of Marsh's hand penetrated Spinelli's shoulder. "Come on, we'll find her."

Spinelli risked a glance at Marsh. His serious eyes matched his voice with no trace of his usual blunt demeanor. Folding the note in half, Spinelli tucked it into his pocket.

Fury rose within Spinelli to a level he'd never experienced before. His emotions spun out of control; the rising heat in his body was enough to melt the remaining ice on the bay just outside the hotel. His hands fisted at his sides and he took a step toward the door leading to the kidnappers before Marsh blocked his path.

"Killing them won't help. I'm guessing they know who has Shannon and Anna. We need them right now to help us find the ladies."

Spinelli knew Marsh was right but the urge to beat some sense into Riordan and Collin would be hard to tamp down.

Marsh kept his feet in place for a few beats, Spinelli assumed, to give him time to calm down a bit and think rationally about his next actions. His penetrating gaze lightened a fragment before he moved aside.

Spinelli stepped into the main living space of the suite. All voices ceased; all gazes landed on him. He felt like a caged animal on display at the zoo. His gaze darted among all parties in the room. Bernie's flaming cheeks supported nearly uncontrollable anger; Davin's pale skin and limp pose indicated pure emotional exhaustion. Collin looked puzzled. Spinelli assumed his brain was working overtime to figure a way to get himself out of this mess. Perhaps he'd try to pin the whole thing on his father and claim some sort of emotional duress.

Riordan's dilated pupils and erratic shifting irises indicated one thing and one thing only, he was simply mad. The Webster Dictionary probably had a picture of Riordan alongside the word madman. With his gaze glued to Riordan, Spinelli moved toward the old man. Knowing one couldn't reason with a crazy person, he considered the option of beating the truth out of Riordan. Weighing the consequences, Spinelli looked away from the crazy old man's hollow, heartless gaze, circled around him and stopped in front of Collin.

Still tied back-to-back in their chairs, Riordan turned his head and stretched his neck to catch a glimpse of what was going on behind him. Spinelli knew if the old man tried hard enough, he could spin his demon head three hundred and sixty degrees, but he still wouldn't be able to see the look in Collin's eyes.

Spinelli strengthened his gaze and inhaled a well-choreographed loud dramatic breath. The shoulder-lifting, chest-inflating, intimidating kind that opened the door for a slow exaggerated exhale through his pursed lips. Leaning forward, he aligned his eyes with Collin's.

"Not a word, Collin. Don't you dare utter one syllable," Riordan snapped.

Collin flinched and lowered his gaze to the floor. Spinelli sunk lower and shifted to put himself in Collin's sightline. Collin let him. His confused gaze softened. "It was two women," he whispered.

"Dammit, son!"

Riordan didn't go ignored. Marsh stepped forward and retuned the gag to Riordan's mouth. The old man growled like a grizzly bear. Marsh tugged on his gag, "You can shut up and live with this or I can get out the duct tape. Your choice." Riordan growled some more and bounced in his chair as if he were having a seizure. Collin's chair vibrated along with him. Marsh placed his foot on the rung of Riordan's chair. "Don't push me."

Spinelli fought for a controlled voice. He hoped to get more information out of Collin. "You said two women took Shannon."

"Yes."

"Did you recognize the women?"

"No, they were wearing Saint Patrick's Day masks and wigs."

"Did they have any unusual or identifiable mannerisms or attributes?"

"Only one of the ladies spoke. She had an Irish accent with a harsh raspy sound to her voice. I'm guessing she's a bit older and smoked most of her life. The other woman never spoke. She just took orders and moved quickly."

"How did they manage to get Shannon and Anna from you guys, and tie you up like this?"

Riordan grunted.

Marsh shot a silencing glare at the crazy old man.

Ignoring his dad, Collin continued. Spinelli figured he hoped for some reprieve on his sentence if he cooperated.

"The older woman had a gun with a silencer. She stood in the kitchenette, in front of the door, and kept the gun pointed at my dad."

"How did they get through the doorway?"

"The same way you guys did, with a keycard."

"A little someone at the front desk made a lot of 'under the table' money today," Walker interjected. "I think I'll go see how much more she knows."

"What happened after they got in the room?" Spinelli continued with the questioning.

"My dad and I were in the living room here waiting for Shannon to get out of the shower when the women barged into the suite. The older woman held the gun on Dad while the other tied me to this chair, then she tied up Dad."

"Shannon was in the shower?"

Collin paused and lowered his gaze. "I think she night have been out of the shower, but she was still in the bathroom getting ready."

"Ready?" Spinelli asked even though he already knew what Collin meant.

"Yes, she needed to get ready to go to the chapel," Collin replied with his gaze glued to the floor.

Though they hadn't made it to the church, the thought of Shannon marrying someone else stung Spinelli's heart with the force of a thousand bees.

"I take it you were going to stand in for your brother today?"

Collin lifted his gaze to meet Spinelli's. "Yeah, we knew Davin didn't have the heart to get it done."

Spinelli shot a glance in Davin's direction. He looked surprised that his brother spoke the words as a compliment to Davin's character rather than an insult. Collin's tone and cooperation alerted Spinelli to the fact that he was done with his father's games as well.

"A forged marriage license and a stand-in groom, that's a union off to a great start. How'd you think you'd get away with this?" Marsh fixed his gaze on Riordan.

Riordan's mouth clamped harder on his gag, Marsh shifted his attention to Collin.

"In our experience, money buys people. We hoped Shannon would get on board."

"And if she didn't?"

"We had motivation. We had Anna. Five years and a male heir was all we wanted. Then Shannon would be free to go with more wealth than she could imagine."

Spinelli's molars gnashed together. "You don't know Shannon," he commented, hardly able to speak the words through his gritted teeth.

"On the contrary, our research indicated Shannon would need just the right motivation, hence Anna."

"Back to the women, you have no idea who they are?"

"That's correct, but from the hate and fury in the old woman's eyes when she eyed my father, I'm guessing they're old acquaintances."

Spinelli shot around the chairs, fixed his gaze on Riordan's, and wrapped his hand around Riordan's throat. He applied just enough pressure to get away with the maneuver without too much harm, yet enough to indicate where the power lay. Riordan's calm pulse thudded against Spinelli's fingertips.

Riordan laughed. Threats were of no use. This madman didn't care about nor fear Spinelli's upper hand. They'd get no information from him, even if they tried to beat it out of him. He'd die before he spoke.

Spinelli released his cramped fingers from Riordan's neck, took a step back and threw his hands in the air before fixing his eyes on Marsh. "We're wasting valuable time here."

Walker shot into the room with the laptop in his hands. He set it on the kitchen table. "I have the surveillance video from the lobby. It shows two women exiting the lobby doors with Shannon and Anna."

Spinelli, Marsh, Bernie, and Davin gathered around the laptop as Walker pressed the play button. The screen showed the profiles of the four women as they entered the lobby from the direction of the elevators, and then their backsides as they exited the lobby into the parking lot. From the angle they watched, it was difficult to read the expressions on Shannon and Anna's faces. From their sluggish steps, Spinelli assumed they had not willingly left with the masked, green-haired ladies.

One of the unknown ladies had her arm slung around Shannon's shoulders. Her white knuckles indicated her firm grip. The woman's other arm was buried in her over-sized handbag, which pushed up against Shannon's side. The other masked woman walked along in the same manner with Anna under her hold. It didn't take a genius to know what was in the handbags encouraging compliance from Shannon and Anna. Too bad there wasn't a video of the parking lot. A vehicle make, model and plate number would be useful.

Bernie leaned forward and asked Walker to play the video again.

"Did you recognize them?" Spinelli asked.

"I'm not sure. I need to see it again."

Everyone slid over to give Bernie full access to the screen. He pulled up a chair, took a seat and aligned his eyes on the center of the monitor. Walker hit the play button. Everyone's attention shifted to Bernie rather than the computer screen. Quietly, they watched him as he studied the short video of the women.

The clip ended. "Play it again," Bernie demanded without moving or shifting his gaze from the screen.

Walker hit play.

Bernie pulled a frown and cocked his head to the side. The video ended and he stared at the blank screen for a moment before he lifted himself from the chair and stepped toward Riordan.

"Bernie, what did you see?" Spinelli asked to deaf ears.

Bernie and Riordan eyed each other for what felt like an eternity to Spinelli.

Everyone edged toward them, waiting for some response.

The corners of Bernie's mouth lifted slowly until a full-fledged smile, stretched nearly from ear to ear. "Well, I'll be dammed. I bet this just burns your ass, you crazy bastard."

Chapter Nine

Maeve sat in her leather chair staring at the two women eating their late breakfast. They seemed like nice ladies. She hated the fact she'd taken them like that and refused to answer their questions, but it was best for everyone except Riordan.

She'd considered consoling the ladies during the drive to Egg Harbor, but successfully fought the urge. She had to keep her abductees fearful of her. If they felt more at ease and planned an escape, it could blow the whole operation.

Maeve cleared her mind of the ladies and allowed it to shift back to Riordan. She recalled the look on his face when she took Shannon from his grasp--priceless, absolutely priceless. The corners of her mouth lifted, and then froze at the thought of all the innocent players in the game.

Maeve shifted her gaze to Brianna, her daughter and co-conspirator. On one hand, she hated to put her daughter in this position but knew she couldn't do the job alone. Brianna willingly offered and she needed a trusted individual to help. She was a good daughter.

In the end, Maeve would lie for Brianna in hopes to get her off scot-free. She didn't mind taking the blame; it would be worth it to see Riordan O'Brien get his due. And how she wanted to be there when he received the official word about his father.

Brianna's fingers danced across the keyboard of her laptop. Maeve wondered what she was looking at as they passed the time. It shouldn't be long now.

"Keep close watch on them, would you? I need to rest my eyes a bit."

Brianna looked up from her laptop and nodded.

"Let me know the second you get word."

Brianna nodded again.

Maeve lifted herself from her chair and limped to the bedroom. She climbed onto the bed, closed her eyes and said a little prayer. She was probably the only person on this earth who thanked God every day for her uncorrected clubfoot. The very foot that ultimately saved her from having to wed Riordan.

When Shannon's mother chose to wed someone else, it had been a landfall for Maeve's father. Francis Quinn quickly stepped in to strike a deal with Emmet, Riordan's dad, for a union of their families. Her father's textile business was going under; an agreement between the Quinn's and O'Brien's could procure financial security for his daughters before word got out about his failing business.

With a bit of coaxing, Francis struck a deal with Emmet that Riordan marry his daughter. Fortunately, for Maeve, Riordan wanted her beautiful, younger, unflawed sister Kathleen. Maeve knew the truth about Riordan. He was an extremist, bordering on crazy. Maeve tried to talk Kathleen out of the union, but Kathleen willingly accepted the task. The O'Brien wealth was too enticing for Kathleen to pass up.

Kathleen and Riordan married and within months, Kathleen admitted her unhappiness with Riordan. His jealous nature wouldn't allow for Kathleen to step out of his sight. If she dared talk to another man, he confined her to the house with no social interaction, not even her own family.

Eight months into their first year of marriage, Kathleen became pregnant but soon miscarried. Maeve thought the stress of living with someone so controlling had contributed to the unfortunate situation.

Within two years of the marriage, Kathleen hired a divorce attorney. Word quickly made its way back to Riordan, and Kathleen suddenly had a change of heart.

During the third year of marriage, Kathleen became pregnant again and had the twins, Davin and Collin. They were not the sons Riordan had dreamed of and Kathleen paid the price. She loved her boys, and it broke her heart to see the way both Riordan and Emmet ignored them.

Before the twins' third birthday, Kathleen was gone. Her death was ruled a suicide, but Maeve new better. Her sister would have never intentionally left her beloved sons to be raised under the confines of Riordan and Emmet.

Riordan had pushed Kathleen from the old footbridge that crossed over the rocky gorge behind their house. Maeve was sure of it; Kathleen wouldn't have jumped on her own. And with her fear of heights, Kathleen would never have attempted to cross the rickety old bridge by herself. Riordan had found the best alibi money could buy.

After the funeral, Riordan allowed no contact between the boys and Kathleen's family. They watched from afar as the boys grew up in an unloving and uncaring home.

Maeve placed her hand over her aching heart. Many times throughout the years, especially those immediately following Kathleen's death, Maeve fought to see the boys. Even the best attorneys were unsuccessful against Emmet and Riordan's wealth and status.

Maeve swiped at the tears that moistened her cheeks and drew in slow deep breaths. Her mind cleared as she entered that place between awake and sleep. Slowly, she drifted off to dreamland. An image of Kathleen's lovely face materialized in her mind, like countless times before, both during Kathleen's time on earth and in her spiritual world.

During the months that followed Kathleen's death, her troubled spirit visited Maeve nearly every night. Though Kathleen could not say it, she hinted to Maeve on more than one visit that her intuition was correct. Riordan had killed her sister that day. He pushed her off the bridge and walked away, leaving Kathleen to die alone on the frigid, unforgiving rocks below.

It had been years since Maeve had dreamed of her sister. Now, Kathleen only made appearances during periods of duress. On one hand, Maeve found it odd how but wasn't too surprised.

Maeve was just twelve years old when her great-grandmother sat her down and explained that her time on earth was nearing the end. Maeve would become responsible for protecting Kathleen who'd been born frail, pure at heart and too trusting. Her great-grandmother insisted that drinking the tea from the dainty ceramic cup would give Maeve the mental fortitude and psychic powers needed to keep a close eye on her naive younger sister.

At the time, Maeve simply appeased the eccentric old woman and drank the strangely concocted herbal tea. It tasted strongly of cinnamon, dill, nuts and basil, yet fruity with grapes and blueberry, while oddly smelling of rose and damp moss.

It didn't take long for Maeve to realize her great-grandmother's concoction actually worked. Maeve's heavy heart not only carried the burden of her own mourning but Kathleen's as well. As they stood side-by-side staring down at their great-grandmother's body during her wake, each tear that swelled in Kathleen's eyes stabbed at Maeve's heart.

Many times throughout their childhood, especially their troubled teen years, Maeve had considered options to undo the spell cast upon her. It was hard enough to manage her own spiraling emotions as a teenager, let alone someone else's as well. But family duty always prevailed, and she'd cast her selfish thoughts aside.

Still, Maeve wondered why her great-grandmother hadn't given Kathleen some sort of crystal ball potion to see her life with Riordan. Surely, had she known she wouldn't have been blinded by the O'Brien wealth and married such a monster. Now Maeve could do nothing except for seek sweet revenge. She knew in her heart, from the very first time her sister's spirit visited her, the only way to free Kathleen's unsettled soul was to take from Riordan the thing that meant the most to him—his wealth.

Maeve's racing heartbeat woke her. She glanced at her watch. She'd only rested for a few minutes. Drawing in slow deep breaths, she calmed the thudding in her chest and her weary eyelids drifted closed again.

Kathleen's flawless milky-white face, framed by her long, flaming-red hair, floated through Maeve's mind with the grace of an angel. A vision of beauty, she appeared just as she was nearly three decades ago. She hadn't aged. How could she? Riordan had taken that option away from her.

Kathleen's bright ruby red lips parted.

Maeve, my dear sister, you've carried this burden of revenge for too long. I see how tired you are. I ask, no matter what happens today, that you let it go, for your own sake. You've done all you can. My sons are grown men and can fend for themselves. As you are well aware, from your distant, yet close watch on my sons all these years, Davin is much like our father: smart, kind and loving. No matter what happens today, he'll be fine.

And Collin, if you could have seen and heard him just a few minutes ago, he's found the goodness that had been stowed away in his heart all along. He's a strong man who will accept the consequences of his actions, and for that, I am very proud. My spirit will now rest knowing the goodness in both my son's hearts. The evil living within Riordan will die along with him someday.

I am so sorry for the curse that had been cast upon you. Again, I ask when you wake to forgive Riordan and free your soul of this burden. Live the rest of your years in happiness, as you deserved all along.

* * * *

Bernie kept his gaze on Riordan. "Well, it appears your little world is about to come crumbling down. I guess old Maeve thinks that revenge is a dish best served cold. And here you thought you'd rid yourself of her years ago," Bernie commented as another satisfying chuckle escaped his lips.

Spinelli watched as the white of Riordan's left eyeball turned red as a fire truck. The bulging must have caused a vessel to break. Spinelli had never seen anyone's eyes protrude as far out of their sockets. Spit saturated Riordan's gag and ran down his chin as he fiercely growled. Bernie had obviously struck a nerve.

Spinelli's mind did a double take. Did Bernie really just use a specific woman's name? Though he still didn't have a clue where Shannon and Anna were, Bernie's sudden change in emotions sent a ripple of relief through Spinelli's veins. They had another lead.

"Maeve?" Spinelli asked.

All eyes were on Bernie as he stepped back from Riordan and faced the group.

"Maeve is Kathleen's sister."

"Kathleen?"

"Our mother. She died when we were young. I don't really even remember her," Collin replied in not much more than a whisper. Spinelli noted the lost, sad look in his eyes.

"So why would Maeve be here today, and why would she take Shannon and Anna?" Spinelli asked as he shifted his gaze between

Collin, Davin, and Bernie, hoping at least one of them had a clue.

Bernie sucked his bottom lip into his mouth and chewed on it for a moment as he flashed a sympathetic look at Davin and then to Collin. Spinelli assumed the information Bernie was about to share would be hurtful to the men.

"Well?"

Bernie sighed and fixed his gaze on Spinelli, ignoring Riordan's rants. "Maeve is Kathleen's older sister. She was a couple of years behind me in school, and Mary's friend. It's my understanding that when Mary wed Shannon's dad, Maeve's father took the opportunity to negotiate a union between Maeve and Riordan." Bernie threw a quick glance in Riordan's direction then returned his gaze. "Riordan wouldn't have anything to do with Maeve because of her disability but he quickly agreed to take Kathleen as his wife."

"The limp?" Marsh questioned.

"Yeah, that's how I knew who she was from the video. That and what little I could see of her face. She was born with a clubfoot."

"So why is she here now?"

Bernie stole another glance at Davin and Collin. Swallowing hard he continued, "Supposedly, Kathleen committed suicide by jumping off an old footbridge that crossed over a gorge on the O'Brien property. Maeve never believed that to be true. She had reason to believe Riordan pushed Kathleen off the bridge and was angry that he got off scot-free."

Davin gasped and fell back onto the chair behind him. His pale skin turned pasty.

"Davin, are you okay?" Collin's frantic voice sounded across the room.

No response.

Walker hurried toward Davin and crouched down. "Are you okay?"

Davin took a second before he leaned forward and scooted out of the chair. He stepped toward Riordan and aligned his eyes with his father's. "It's true, isn't it?"

Riordan's intense, psychotic glare looked as if it could bore a hole through his son. Davin shook his head, stepped back and looked up at Bernie. "So you think she's here to serve up some justice to my dad by preventing the wedding, in order to hit him where it will hurt him the

104

most?"

"Yep, right in the old pocketbook. If she's able to keep Shannon from Riordan until after Emmet dies, she will have prevailed. Riordan will be broke." Bernie paused, tilted his head to the side and gave a slight shrug. "Of course, so will you guys."

Davin walked over to his brother, "What do you think?"

"It's about time someone socked it to him. I'm sick of living this way."

Davin shot Spinelli a glance. "I'd like to untie my brother."

Spinelli nodded, sure Collin wouldn't be a problem any longer. But he would see to it that Collin got what was coming to him for his role in this whole ordeal, forced or not by his crazy father. The word 'crazy' latched onto Spinelli like a leech. A surge of panic shot through his veins. What if Maeve was as crazy as Riordan? Nobody in this hotel suite, at present, really knew her. If Emmet actually didn't pass in the near future, how far would Maeve be willing to go to serve her revenge on Riordan? After hearing of Maeve's years of bottled-up frustration, Spinelli feared Shannon's life might still be in serious jeopardy.

Spinelli fixed his gaze on Bernie. "So do you really think Maeve will simply let Shannon and Anna walk the second Emmet dies?"

Bernie inhaled a deep breath and let it out slowly as he pondered Spinelli's question. He shook his head. "I can't really say for sure. I can only assume and hope. She's a nice, good-hearted person. At least she was years ago." Bernie shot a glance at Riordan, "But Riordan does have a way of bringing out the worst in in person."

The air drained from Spinelli's lungs and a sharp pain shot through his heart as if someone had stuck a knife through it and twisted.

"And what happens if Emmet doesn't die soon?" Bernie asked, his voice trailing off to nearly a whisper.

Marsh pulled up a chair in front of the laptop and rapidly pounded the keys. Within moments, his fingers stilled. "She's a rookie."

"What did you find?" Spinelli asked as he leaned over Marsh's shoulder to catch a glimpse of the screen.

"Credit card use at a resort in Egg Harbor."

"From when?"

"Last night, and less than an hour ago."

"Punch the address in and Walker and I will run up there. You can hang back here and hold tight," Spinelli instructed as he handed Marsh his phone, hoping Marsh wouldn't notice his shaky fingers. He worked to regulate his thudding heart, which beat as if it were pumping peanut butter through his veins. Though he was one-step closer to Shannon, a hint of fear swirled in his stomach at the thought of the rug being pulled from under his feet again. It was a legitimate possibility, just like when he thought he'd find her in the room in which they were now standing.

Walker hopped into the driver's seat. Spinelli was glad to climb into the passenger seat, knowing he'd probably press the accelerator to the floor if he were behind the wheel. Walker pulled into traffic. Orange barricades, closing off streets for the parade route, blocked nearly every turn. The phone's GPS did not register the alternate route. He fought the urge to chuck it out the window. Finally, Walker found a route to the highway and they headed north to Egg Harbor. According to the GPS, the trip would take twenty-two minutes. It would be the longest twenty-two minutes of his life.

Once on the highway, Spinelli's hands stopped shaking but he couldn't fight the perspiration beading on his upper lip and temples. He swiped his hand across his face, and then over his thighs.

"She's okay. I don't believe for a moment this Maeve person has any intention of hurting her," Walker stated as he kept his eyes focused on the road. Walker always appeared calm, his expression neutral, even in the worst of situations. Of course, it was never Walker's wife who was friends with murdered Santa's, elves or lovers. It was never Walker's wife who'd been taken hostage by drug-dealing thugs, and psychotic men or women. Walker lived the good life, a regular life, with a wife and two young kids at home who never found themselves in this kind of mess.

What was it about him and Shannon that caused all this craziness? Perhaps they just weren't good for one another. *Did I really just think that?* He nearly proposed to her on Valentine's Day, and had pulled the ring out of his dresser drawer at least a thousand times since then just to imagine what it might look like on her finger. Earlier in the day, he kicked himself for not marrying her. If he had, she wouldn't be in this mess. He swiped his sweaty palms over his thigh again. "Dammit."

"What?"

"Nothing, I just want to get there. I just want to know she's okay." Spinelli closed his eyes and inhaled a deep breath.

"I know you do."

Spinelli fixed his gaze on Walker. "I'm going to marry her."

Walker risked a glance away from the road. "I know you are. Jeana and I have known all along. Christ, even Marsh figured it out. Mad Dog calls me at least once a week to make sure he doesn't miss the wedding. Captain Jackson prays for the miracle that you figure it out before she retires so she knows you'll be taken care of when she's gone." Walker chuckled. "We're all just waiting for you to shit or get off the pot."

"Walker?"

"Yeah?"

"Put the pedal down, would you?"

Breaking the rules, Walker pressed down on the accelerator and turned the twenty-two minute trip into fifteen.

With a quick flash of his badge, Spinelli secured the room number associated to Maeve's credit card from the nice lady behind the counter.

They drove over the winding road to the third condo building. Spinelli leaped out of the car before Walker cut the engine. He sprinted down the hall with Walker on his heels, halting on a dime in front of room 225.

Spinelli pulled the keycard from his pocket. The engagement ring he carried with him came out as well. He lost himself in the sparkle of it for a moment. It would be on her finger, momentarily.

"That's very nice there buddy, but we should get in there so you can give it to her."

Walker knocked on the door.

Spinelli's heart thudded in his chest. He was ready. Excitement ripped through him with the crack of a whip.

Silence.

Walker rapped his knuckle on the door again.

Nothing.

Shear panic stung at Spinelli's core. He stuffed the ring back into his pocket and drew his weapon as Walker slid the keycard into the slot. They bounded through the doorway to find Shannon and Anna seated at the kitchen table. A woman wearing a green wig and mask dropped her weapon at Spinelli's command and threw her hands into the air. The second woman held her hand into the air, palm facing Spinelli, as if to indicate he should shut up and wait a moment. Her other hand clutched the cellphone pressed to her ear.

Walker cuffed the first woman as Spinelli moved toward the female with the cell.

The woman dropped the phone and collapsed into the chair behind her, her body limp.

"Mom!" the cuffed woman yelled in concern. Walker kept his grip on her.

"Hands in the air," Spinelli barked.

The woman in the chair slowly raised her hands as if the weight of them was too much to bear.

He edged toward her. "Are you okay?"

No response.

"Maeve?"

The woman sucked in a labored breath. "Yes, I'm fine, it's done. Emmet's dead."

Out of the corner of his eye, Spinelli caught a glimpse of Walker bending over to pick up the other woman's weapon.

"It's fake."

"What?"

"The gun is a fake," Walker repeated as he holstered his weapon.

These ladies weren't going to hurt anyone. They only intended to strip Riordan of his inheritance. Bernie was right; they took Shannon and Anna so Riordan couldn't have them.

Shannon cried Spinelli's name. He hurried toward her, freed her wrist from the cuff. She leaped up into his arms, putting a death-grip around his neck. He couldn't blame her and he didn't mind. She'd been through a lot in the past twenty-plus hours. Her body shook and her tears saturated the collar of his jacket.

Loosening her grip, she inched back and looked up at him. He lost himself in the depth of the sea of green holding his gaze.

"I was so afraid I would never see you again," she squeaked out between her gasps.

He had no words for her; he'd felt the same so many times throughout the past twenty-four hour period. The lump in his throat wouldn't budge. He could tell by the relieved, yet desperate look in her eyes she needed to hear something from him right now but he just couldn't seem to speak.

Cupping her head in his hands, he swiped his thumbs over her wet cheeks. Her pleading eyes tugged at his heart. "I'm so sorry I didn't find you sooner. I'm so sorry I didn't protect you, I …" his voice trailed off, abandoning him again.

Shannon reached up and pressed the tip of her index finger to his lips. "Without you, who knows where I'd be right now."

His vision blurred as her loving gaze reassured him of everything he needed to know. Her soft fingertip traced his lips. With her face still cupped in his hands, he tilted her head back, brushed his lips across her sweet, smooth, velvety lips, and captured her exhausted sigh. Every bone in his body heated to near boiling at her simple touch. Her warm, welcoming mouth pulled him further into her being, any further and they'd become one. It was time. He would reach into his pocket, pull out the ring he'd bought over a month ago, take a knee and propose to her right now. His steady hand drifted to his side.

"I hate to interrupt, but by any chance could I get un-handcuffed from this table?" Anna asked.

Spinelli spun around to meet her pleading brown eyes. He'd nearly forgotten anyone else was in the room. "Yes, crap, I'm sorry Anna."

Walker was busy with Maeve and her daughter.

Spinelli pulled the cuff from Anna's wrist. She rubbed it as he helped her to her feet. Spinelli shifted toward Shannon again but halted when Anna cleared her throat. "Hey, where's mine?"

Spinelli cocked his head to the side and arched a brow. Knowing exactly what she meant, he asked the question anyhow. "Where's your what?" He could tease too. Months ago, if not for Anna's little shove, he and Shannon may have never hooked up.

Anna's wicked smile grew as she pointed at Shannon. "She got all this smoldering, eyeing-up and lip-smacking stuff. All I get is 'sorry, let me help you up'?"

"Please forgive my rudeness, Anna," Spinelli responded as he

109

stepped toward her, gave her a peck on the cheek and pulled her into a quick but firm hug.

Anna took a step back but kept her curious gaze on him.

Spinelli pulled a frown. "What?"

"Nice hat. And I'm just curious, what did you have to do for those beads."

Spinelli had forgotten he wore the ridiculous green crochet leprechaun hat with the black band, gold buckle and flaps over his ears. He'd forgotten about the green beads as well.

Anna giggled.

"Now what?"

"Well, it just occurred to me that in the recent past, I've seen pictures of you dressed as Santa Claus and Cupid. With just a few more slight adjustments to your current wardrobe, you'd be dressed as a full-fledged leprechaun today. A rather tall one, but a leprechaun nonetheless." Anna paused and shot a quick glance to Shannon before returning her gaze to Spinelli. "With actions like that, I'd say you're a man in love. I'm already curious to see how you'll look next month dressed in a big, fluffy bunny costume with floppy ears."

Though they all shared a laugh at Anna's comment, a blanket of fear wrapped around Spinelli. He wasn't sure he had the strength to endure another holiday crisis with Shannon. Racing to save and protect her had taken its toll on him, but he couldn't live without her. Perhaps he could petition to cancel Easter. Anxiety coiled in his stomach. What if Shannon decided *she* didn't have the strength to endure another holiday crisis with him? They'd set quite the track record already: two murders, an attempted murder and two counts of kidnapping at Christmas time; four murders and a suicide on Valentine's Day; and technically speaking, four counts of kidnapping, two counts each for both Shannon and Anna, during the Saint Patrick's Day weekend celebration. On a good note, each crisis seemed to lighten up a bit with the current holiday. Maybe by Easter they'd only have to deal with a stolen Easter basket. He could only hope.

Chapter Ten

Spinelli and Walker drove back to the Harbor Resort in Sturgeon Bay with Maeve and Brianna in the back seat. Shannon and Anna followed in Maeve's rental. It killed Spinelli not to be with Shannon but for security purposes, he thought it best to keep a close watch on Maeve and her daughter. They couldn't all fit in either car. He must have checked his rear view mirror at least a thousand times to make sure Shannon and Anna were behind them.

Though she was about to face the consequence associated with kidnapping, Maeve's eyes still radiated with pleasure. She'd soon be able to serve up her dish of revenge on Riordan.

Walker worked his way through Sturgeon Bay's downtown streets. It was a bit easier now that the parade was finished, but an entire city of people dressed in green still saturated the sidewalks in front of the downtown bars, restaurants, and shops. Evidently, the Saint Patrick's Day event was an all-day occurrence in this community.

Walker parked near the lobby doors of the hotel. Shannon pulled up alongside them.

The roar of laughter met them as soon as they stepped through the entrance of the hotel. Glancing in the direction of the bar, Spinelli could see only one green mass of people.

One set of fingers wove firmly among Shannon's soft, warm fingers, and his other hand wrapped around Maeve's arm, just above her elbow. They all continued toward Riordan's suite. The bounce in Maeve's step actually pulled Spinelli along. She'd waited a long time to serve Riordan his due justice, and Spinelli wanted to let her before he turned her over to the local authorities.

The basketball game on the television was the only noise Spinelli heard when they entered the suite. Marsh and Bernie sat at the kitchen table, Davin and Collin each sat in one of the leather chairs in the living room area and Riordan was still bound and gagged in his chair. All eyes shifted from the game to Spinelli and his group.

Bernie sprang off his chair and pulled Shannon into a big bear hug. "I'm so glad to see you. Are you okay?" he asked as he stepped back and scanned her from top to bottom.

"I'm fine. They didn't really do anything to us."

Bernie hugged her again before stepping aside to let everyone else pass through the small kitchen area. It took only a moment for Maeve and Riordan to lock gazes. The completely satisfied grin on Maeve's face caused the veins on Riordan's neck and forehead to bulge. His fire engine red cheeks likely raised the temperature in the room a few degrees. Maeve didn't need to speak, for Riordan to know why she looked so pleased. He yelled something but the gag he wore muffled the unidentifiable words.

Maeve edged closer to Riordan as she pulled out the phone she'd swiped from him earlier in the day. Her smile was unstoppable. "Riordan, how nice it is to see you today. It's been a while." She paused and leaned forward, aligning her eyes with his furious gaze. Riordan's dagger-shooting look might have killed a lesser woman.

"I have your phone here. It appears you missed a very important call today," Maeve said gleefully as she danced his phone in front of his eyes.

Maeve's voice, the one that radiated exhaustion less than an hour ago, now exuded strength and confidence.

Riordan squirmed in his chair and tugged to free his arms from their bindings. The psychotic look in his eyes sent a shiver up Spinelli's spine.

Maeve edged a bit closer to Riordan. "Hmm, it seems you missed the call from your dear old dad's lawyer." She paused for emphasis. "I'm so sorry to be the one to tell you, but Emmet passed a little less than an hour ago."

Riordan growled and bounced in his chair. The blood vessels in his right eye popped, filling the white of his eye with red. Now both eyes matched his cheeks.

An evil laugh flowed from Maeve. "I can't begin to image what Emmet's money will buy for the university."

Riordan gasped as if he'd just been freed from nearly drowning. His body convulsed briefly before his eyes rolled back into his head, and then his head fell forward. His body stilled.

Marsh dialed 911 as Spinelli felt for a pulse; faint, but it was there.

Davin and Collin, along with everyone else, watched as the EMTs rolled Riordan out on a stretcher.

"I'm so glad he didn't die," Maeve whispered to Brianna.

Spinelli knew Maeve only wanted Riordan to live so she could watch him live out his days penniless. Nobody reacted to her comment.

Maeve turned to the twins. Her loving gaze absorbed theirs. "First of all, I want you to know that I am truly sorry if any of this caused you pain or sorrow. You are my nephews, my dear sister's children, and I love you both. I'm sure you are probably a little concerned about your finances since your grandfather has left all his money and possessions to the university. I want you to know right now, you'll be taken care of and have no need to worry."

Spinelli watched as Davin just stared at his aunt. He looked confused, perhaps even shocked. Why wouldn't he though? He'd been handed a lot to deal with. His grandfather died, his dad nearly died, and he was now penniless. Collin seemed less puzzled by the events that just took place. In fact, Spinelli thought he'd seen a tinge of relief pass through his squinty little eyes. Odd, since Collin was in a heap of trouble. But maybe the inadvertent release from his father and grandfather's psychotic hold was worth the punishment he'd likely soon undergo.

Collin raised a brow. "Why don't we have to worry?"

Maeve smiled warmly and placed her hand to Davin's cheek, then Collin's. "Your mother loved you so much. Even with the risk that Riordan and Emmet would find out, she squirreled some cash away while married to you father--in the event you would need it someday."

"What?" Collin asked.

"She tucked away some cash for you," Maeve repeated

"How, where?" he mumbled.

"It's my understanding that when your father gave her money to go to town, she'd shop frugally and tuck some of the cash aside."

Collin's face scrunched, "Well, she couldn't have tucked that much away."

Maeve nodded. "You're right, it was a just couple of thousand here or there until the day before her death. That day, she somehow found a way to withdraw two million dollars from one of Emmet's accounts, or his safe. I don't really know which, and I don't have a clue as to how she accomplished the task. I knew from the look in her eyes when she handed me the cash, I didn't dare ask." Tears filled Maeve's eyes as she took a moment. Everyone waited out her pause. "Less than twenty four hours after taking the cash, your mother died." Maeve placed her hand over her heart. "I'm sorry, but there's no way your mother killed herself that day. She wouldn't have. She loved you both too much to leave you alone with Riordan and Emmet."

Maeve waited for the twins to say something. After a few beats of silence, she filled the gap. "My late husband, your uncle whom I'm sure you don't even remember, invested your money nearly three decades ago. Let me just say, he was a wiz with cash. You and your heirs will have no financial worries in the future. However, since the money is in my possession, it will be doled out to you in healthy increments. In the event any portion, no matter how miniscule, is given to or used to support Riordan, you'll be cut off. He killed your mother. I know it in my heart," Maeve finished with conviction.

Spinelli figured when Riordan heard news of his son's non-shareable wealth he'd surely blow a gasket, probably have a heart attack and die right there on the spot.

Chapter Eleven

Spinelli sunk into the deep leather chair in his hotel room, pulling Shannon onto his lap along the way. No suite for them, just a simple room. All he ever needed from this day forward was she. She leaned her head against his shoulder; her slow even breaths warmed his neck. She molded to him, fitting perfectly.

It didn't surprise him that it took only seconds for her to fall asleep. She'd had quite the couple of days.

He inhaled deeply and took in the tantalizing scent of her fiery-red hair. The fragrance reminded him of a bright spring morning. He pressed his lips lightly to her forehead. She didn't even stir. Her milky-white skin looked heavenly to him. Not wanting to wake her, he fought the urge to reach up and run his fingers over her soft, smooth cheek.

Though she looked tiny and frail in his arms, he knew differently. She had a strong will and was completely capable of getting through any situation thrown at her.

Spinelli glanced at the clock and understood his weariness as well. It was nearly midnight. Within minutes, it would be Shannon's birthday.

The hours spent with the Sturgeon Bay Police and Door County Sheriff's Departments had been painfully draining. He'd just wanted to get Shannon out of there and into his arms so she could rest.

Anna now rested in the adjoining room with Marsh on the opposite side and Walker across the hall. Anna seemed to take the unfortunate situation like a real trooper. He had known from the first day they met, she was one tough old cookie.

Valerie J. Clarizio

Spinelli gazed at Shannon's angelic face and wondered how he'd become the luckiest man in the world. He considered pinching himself to make sure he wasn't lost in a dream.

He reached up, pulled Shannon's note from his shirt pocket, and carefully, and quietly, unfolded it before he set it on the wide arm of the chair. His heart picked up pace as he read the letter in its entirety. Though Shannon now rested securely in his arms, he couldn't seem to tamp down the renewed anger rising in him as he read the words of her abduction and separation from Anna. Within moments, pride swept his entire being and pushed the anger aside. He re-read the section of Shannon's near escape and her will to try again. His stomach fluttered, his heart swelled, and his core warmed as the last paragraph of her letter replayed in his mind over and over.

Nick, in the event I don't see you again, please know that I love you now and always. You are the one I wanted to grow old with. I will carry you forever in my heart, soul and spirit. Nick Spinelli, you are the strongest, most loving person I know. I will forever pray for your happiness and health.
Love, Shannon

Caving to his selfishness, Spinelli lifted his hand and combed his fingers through Shannon's smooth, silky strands of hair before his hand came to rest against her warm, inviting, cheek. Her eyes fluttered open but quickly closed again. He tilted her head slightly for better access to her soft, irresistible lips. He touched them lightly with his before he pulled his head back in hopes to catch a glimpse of her beautiful emerald eyes. It took but a moment for her lids to rise, and the sea of green staring back at him instantly swallowed him whole.

Wasting no time, he dipped his head and fully took her mouth. The heat of her tongue nearly set him to flames. Her fingers wove through his hair; his hand cupped a breast through her shirt. Her back still pinned one arm between her and the chair. As if reading his mind, she shifted her position more upright, freeing his arm and his hand for roaming. He nearly chuckled at her mind-reading skills in the few short months they'd been together. At this rate, he'd soon have no private thoughts left.

Her scorching tongue turned his mind to mush. She sent every nerve ending in his body to the highest point of arousal he'd ever experienced. He couldn't think anymore. He could only react and deepened his kiss.

Straddling him in the chair, she placed her hands on his cheeks and locked her smoldering gaze onto his. He needed a crowbar to tear his gaze from hers, as he glanced at her letter still on the arm of the chair. Unless she saw it in the last few seconds, she would have no way of knowing he'd seen the letter she wrote to him. Shifting his gaze back to her, he found her looking at the paper. Her breath held for a moment.

The sheer intensity of her concentrated gaze bored into his soul. "I meant every word of it, Nick."

A thrill snapped through him like a lightning bolt as if this information was new to him. Deep down he'd known it for a while, but the letter confirmed his suspicions. Hearing her say the words, with such sincerity and assurance, rendered him speechless. His heart pounded in his chest.

Shannon's green eyes darkened as she leaned forward and pressed her fiery-hot and needy lips to his. Spinelli's greedy hands went to work, pulling her shirt up and over her head so quickly their lips hardly parted to complete the task. His fingers loosened the hook on her bra, freeing her small perky round breasts from their confinement.

Pulling his lips from hers, he fastened his mouth around one breast as he cupped the other in the palm of his hand. Her breath hitched and released with a soft moan. If that was the last sound he ever heard, he'd die a happy man. She had the most beautiful breasts.

Shannon's small hands floated down and fluidly worked the button and zipper of his jeans. If she took any longer, the force of his erection would take care of that task.

He somehow found enough sense to lift himself to his feet with Shannon in his arms. Her legs wrapped around his waist. He took the four steps needed before playfully tossing her onto the bed. Kneeling before him, she tugged at his jeans as he pulled his shirt over his head. She eyed his erection. He always loved how she looked at him. Only two things were better. Yep, wrapping her mouth around him was one. Her sizzling tongue slid around and over the tip of him before taking him in completely. The escalating pressure was nearly more than he could bear and she'd hardly started. His pulse pounded in his ears as his aching body begged for release. His concentrated effort to hold out nearly failed him as she freed him from the depths of her knowing mouth.

Shannon scooted up on the bed. Her skin flushed at his gaze. He tugged her jeans and panties from her before he crawled up beside her. Before he knew it, his mouth covered hers, probing, exploring, as if it had never been there before. He was ready, so ready to dip inside her velvet opening.

He pulled back to look at her. Her emerald gaze studied him. He caught a glimpse of the sparkle on her finger. She hadn't noticed yet that he'd slipped the diamond ring on her finger while she slept. He shivered; he couldn't breathe. His eyes watered. Shear panic flashed in her eyes. *For crissake, Spinelli, pull yourself together. You're scaring her.*

* * * *

Shannon froze in reaction to Spinelli's abrupt move away from her during one of the most heated moments of their lovemaking to date. Had she done something wrong? Panic ripped through her as she studied him. In an instant, his olive colored skin turned ghostly white. His body shook, his breath held to the point that his skin took on a blue hue. Were those tears in his charcoal-gray eyes?

Spinelli didn't move, didn't breathe, and just kept staring at her.

Shannon propped herself up on her right elbow and placed her left hand against his cheek, "Are you okay, Nick?"

His jaw moved slightly but no words escaped.

"Nick."

He flinched at the sound of his name, as if she'd branded him with a red-hot poker, but with his abrupt movement, she caught a glimpse of the heart shaped diamond ring on her finger. Pulling her hand from his face, she centered it in front of her eyes. A thrill snapped though her. Her heart thudded in her chest. She imagined her watery gaze now matched his. The ring she stared at certainly beat out a 14-karat gold Claddagh friendship ring. This Saint Patrick's Day adventure had been more than she bargained for, in more ways than one.

Catching her breath, she glanced back at Nick. He still looked sick. The words she wished to speak scrambled in her head. They were quite the pair. She needed to say something soon, before he suffocated himself. "Does this mean ..." Shannon swallowed the infringing excitement in her throat that threatened to block her speech. "Are you asking ...?"

Shannon's words halted as Nick's began. "Yes, I'm asking that you marry me."

"Yes, Nick Spinelli. I will marry you."

His smoldering gaze turned black as coal at her response. He leaned toward her and captured her lips with his hot, hungry mouth. The immeasurable possessiveness of his kiss overwhelmed her. Heat spiraled through her body, her skin on the verge of melting. The sensations ripping through her could only be described as pure pleasure, and he was just getting started. *A lifetime of this.* She pulled him tighter to her desperate aching body. *Oh, Yeah.*

About the Author

Valerie Clarizio lives in beautiful Door County Wisconsin with her husband and extremely spoiled cat. She loves to read, write, and spend time at her cabin in the Upper Peninsula of Michigan. She's lived her life surrounded by men, three brothers, a husband, and a male Siamese cat who required his own instruction manual. Keeping up with all the men in her life has turned her into a successful hunter and fisherwoman. She holds a Master of Business Administration degree and works as a Finance Director. She is a member of Romance Writers of America and the Wisconsin Romance Writers of America.

Twitter:@VClarizio
https://www.facebook.com/Valerie.Clarizio
http://valclarizio.wordpress.com/

Other works by the author with Melange Books

Covert Exposure, A Nick Spinelli Mystery
Craving Vengeance, A Nick Spinelli Mystery

Love Thaws a Frozen Heart, in the FROZEN ANTHOLOGY